BABYSITTERS' WINTER HOLIDAY

The four of us were standing, shivering, in the car-park when Dawn and Mallory arrived, and a few minutes later, Stacey.

"We're all here!" I said. "The Babysitters Club is here and ready to go."

"Ready for a week of fun," said Stacey.

"A week of contests," said Kristy.

"A week of reading and lounging," I said. "I'm going to turn into the Leicester Lodge Lounge Lizard."

. . . at that moment, a huge cheer rose up in the car-park.

"The coaches are here!" someone shouted.

My friends and I turned to look. Goodbye, Connecticut, I thought. Hello, Vermont!

Every year Stoneybrook Middle School is invited to Leicester Lodge for a week of winter fun. What with babysitting and winter sports, this looks set to be a trip like no other. And if it doesn't stop snowing soon, the Babysitters Club might be snowbound till Spring!

Also in the Babysitters Club series:

Look out for:

Babysitter Specials

BABYSITTERS' WINTER HOLIDAY

Ann M. Martin

Hippo Books
Scholastic Children's Books
London

Scholastic Children's Books
Scholastic Publications Ltd,
7-9 Pratt Street, London NW1 0AE

Scholastic Inc.,
730 Broadway, New York, NY 10003, USA

Scholastic Canada Ltd,
123 Newkirk Road, Richmond Hill,
Ontario, Canada L4C 3G5

Ashton Scholastic Pty Ltd,
P O Box 579, Gosford, New South Wales,
Australia

Ashton Scholastic Ltd,
Private Bag 1, Penrose, Auckland,
New Zealand

First published by Scholastic Publications Inc., 1989
First published in the UK by Scholastic Publications Limited, 1991

ISBN 0 590 76631 7

THE BABY-SITTERS CLUB is a trademark of Scholastic Inc.

Typeset in Plantin by AKM Associates (UK) Ltd, Southall, London
Printed by Cox & Wyman Ltd, Reading, Berks

10 9 8 7 6 5 4 3 2 1

For L.G.

Mary Anne's Magical
Winter Adventure
A Book for Logan

Our magical winter
adventure is about to
begin! Tomorrow everyone
in Stoneybrook Middle
School will board coaches
and travel to Leicester
Lodge in Hooksett Crossing,
Vermont, for five whole
days. Actually more like

five-and-a-half days.
We leave on Monday
morning and come back
on Saturday afternoon.
The lodge is huge and
beautiful. (I know because
we go there every year.)
It's actually a gigantic
hotel, and it's in the
mountains in an area
with plenty of snow,
which makes it the perfect
place for... Winter Carnival!
I had tons of fun there
last year and the year
before, even though I
didn't want to be part
of the Winter War.

Going to Leicester
Lodge is ~~compulsory~~. That
means everyone has to go
unless, like you, ~~Logan~~,
someone has a really,
really good excuse not to.
Even if the trip weren't
compulsory, I'd want
to go. I like having
time for reading and
just being with my

friends.   Also, this
year, I volunteered
to be the trip historian
and do research on
Leicester Lodge and
Hooksett Crossing.
Anyone who volunteers
for a special role on
the trip gets extra
marks in school.
I'm also going to write
this book about my
adventure and give it
to you, since you
couldn't come. Your family
has had that trip to
Aruba planned for ages.
I really wish you could
have come to the lodge
with us, but since you
can't, well, now you can
read about our week
in Vermont.
So, Logan, this book
is for you from me,
            Mary Anne.

1st CHAPTER

Mary Anne

Sunday night

I don't believe it. They almost cancelled our trip this afternoon! The head and our teachers, I mean. That's because the weather reports for Vermont have been so bad. Lots of snow is on the way. Even here in Stoneybrook we had a little snow this weekend, which I guess is why the head panicked.

Anyway, the rumour about the cancellation started this morning,

5

and by this afternoon, so many parents were phoning the head (at his home) to find out if it was true that around 6:00 he phoned in an announcement to WSTO saying, "Despite weather reports, the Stoneybrook Middle School trip and Winter Carnival are still on...."

Thank goodness we were still going to the lodge. I'd have died if I couldn't have finished my book for Logan. By Sunday, he had already left for Aruba, and if our trip had been cancelled, not only would we have had to go to school instead of to the lodge, but the week would have seemed a year long without him. In Vermont I'd be distracted by all the new things to do. In Connecticut, I would just have moped around. Of course, the best thing would have been if Logan could have come to Vermont with us. (He's never been on the trip because his family were still living in Kentucky last year.) But you can't have everything.

Anyway, by Sunday night the rumour had been cleared up (or put to rest, as my father would say), so despite the overcast sky and the light snow that was falling, I went to bed knowing the trip was still on.

The trip really is a pretty amazing thing. I don't think kids in many middle schools do what we do every year—go away for almost a week at practically no cost. Our parents are just asked to make a donation to the Winter Carnival Fund. If we don't collect enough money, then the Leicester Lodge people cover whatever isn't raised. A nice (rich) couple owns the lodge, and they do this for lots of schools all winter long, just so that pupils can have an away-from-home experience. It's something they like to do for kids. And they really make our experience enjoyable! Several wings of their huge lodge are fitted out as comfortable dormitories. (Usually, more than one school is at the lodge at the same time, which is fun because you get to meet new people.) And all week long, they feed us terrific food, and let us use the lodge along with the skiers and other people who are holidaying there. They don't even mind our Winter War.

Before I get too much further along, I'd better stop and tell you who I am. I'm Mary Anne Spier. I'm thirteen and I'm in the eighth grade at the Stoneybrook Middle School (SMS). I don't have any brothers or sisters, just an adorable grey kitten named Tigger. I don't have a mum, either, but I do have a pretty nice dad. We live in Stoneybrook, Connecticut, and I have a lot of friends here. Most of them are my friends in the Babysitters Club. There's also Logan (who's part of the club too.) He's my boyfriend. It was a long time before I felt brave enough to call him that, but that's what he is.

My friends in the Babysitters Club are Kristy Thomas, Dawn Schafer, Claudia Kishi, Stacey McGill, Jessi Ramsey, and Mallory Pike. They were all going on this trip, too. For weeks, the seven of us had been so excited we could hardly say the words "Winter Carnival" without becoming hysterical. Five of us had been on the trip before, but Mal and Jessi hadn't, since they're in the sixth grade. It would be their first time.

Kristy and Dawn are my two best friends. Kristy is outgoing and has a big mouth, but I don't mind her mouth—much. She's funny and full of good ideas. She comes from a huge, mixed-up family with brothers, a stepbrother and stepsister, and even an adopted sister. Dawn is an individual. She has somehow learned not to care about what people think, and to just go her own way and do what she wants to do, without hurting anyone's feelings. Dawn has one brother, who lives in California with her father. (Her parents are divorced.)

Claudia and Stacey are best friends, but not *my* best friends, although we're all pretty close. They're both trendy dressers, and definitely the most sophisticated of the club members. Stacey even grew up in New York City. One thing you should know about Stacey is that she has diabetes, but she copes really well. Claudia is an artist and a junk-food addict. Stacey's parents are in the middle of a divorce; Claudia's aren't. Stacey is an only child; Claud has an older sister named Janine.

Then there are Jessi and Mal who, by Sunday night, were getting nervous about the trip to the lodge. It wasn't their first time away from home (we all went to Camp Mohawk for two weeks in the summer), but the sixth-graders are always the "babies" of the trip, going away with the "big kids" and that's not an easy position to be in. Anyway, Jessi and Mal are also best friends, and they're big readers, but that's where the similarities end. Mal wants to be a writer when she grows up; Jessi is a talented ballet dancer. Mal has seven younger brothers and sisters; Jessi has two. Also, Mal is white and Jessi is black.

Those are my friends, and I was glad they were all going on the trip with me. (I would have been even happier if Logan were going, though.) At least the trip hadn't been called off. I have to admit that I was rather surprised by that. When I woke up on Monday the sky was the colour of lead, and the air was heavy with moisture. It was 28° outside, according to our thermometer— perfect snowing weather. And when I tuned into the weather channel on TV, the reports for Vermont were grimmer than ever.

"You'd better turn on the radio, Mary Anne," Dad said to me. "If the trip is off, the cancellation will be announced."

But there was no cancellation, just the report from the night before saying that the trip was still on.

"It's on!" I shouted to Dad.

A good thing too, since I was dressed, packed, and ready to go.

As soon as Dad and I had finished breakfast, I jumped up from the table and said, "Okay, are you ready to leave?"

"For school?" Dad replied. "Now?"

"Yes."

"It's too early. You'll have to wait for at least

Mary anne

half an hour once you reach the school car-park.
And it's not even thirty degrees outside."

"I know," I said. "Only twenty-eight. *Please*
can't we go? I don't think I can wait a second
longer."

"Well, all right," Dad answered. "Brush your
teeth and say goodbye to Tigger."

I refrained from reminding him that I'm not a
baby. Instead, I just brushed my teeth and then
picked up Tigger. All I had to do was look into
those shiny eyes of his and I wanted to cry. I could
feel a huge lump in my throat.

"Mew?" said Tigger.

"I'll be back on Saturday," I told him. "That's
a promise." Then I kissed him on his furry head
and set him on the floor. " 'Bye, Tigger."

Tigger went tearing after a plastic ball with a
bell in it. He had no idea what was going on.

"Don't forget to feed him," I told Dad about
twelve times as we drove through Stoneybrook to
SMS. "And change his water. And put that
ointment in his eyes if they start to run. And
check behind the fridge when his toys are
missing."

"Yes, ma'am," Dad said good-naturedly.

When he turned the car into the car-park, I
could see that I wasn't the only one who was
excited and had wanted to arrive early. About
thirty other kids were there, including Kristy,
Claudia, and Jessi. I said a nervous goodbye to

11

Dad, hauled my stuff out of the car, and joined my friends. Like me, they were each carrying two rucksacks—except for Claud. Claud was laden down with rucksacks as well as her skiing equipment. She is virtually a champion at skiing.

"Doesn't the lodge lend us skis and boots?" I asked. (Not that I was about to go skiing. I'm the world's most unathletic person.)

"Yes," Claud replied, "but I wanted to bring my own stuff this year. I ski better with it. And I plan to help lead the Red Team to victory in the Winter War."

"No you won't!" cried Kristy. "The Blue Team is going to win!"

The Winter War, I should explain, is the main activity of the Winter Carnival up at the lodge. The week before we left for Vermont, everyone in our school had been randomly assigned to either the Red Team or the Blue Team. The teams would compete in five events during Winter Carnival—an ice-skating contest, a snowball fight, a snow sculpture contest, a downhill skiing competition, and a cross-country skiing competition. Although going to Vermont is compulsory, participating in the war is not. (Thank heavens. I didn't plan to join in—even though I wanted my team, the Blue Team, to win.) In case you couldn't tell, Kristy and Claudia were in opposite teams. Kristy was even the *captain* of her team. It was going to be a very competitive week for her.

The four of us were standing, shivering, in the car-park when Dawn and Mallory arrived, and a few minutes later, Stacey.

"We're all here!" I said. "The Babysitters Club is here and ready to go."

"Ready for a week of fun," said Stacey.

"A week of contests," said Kristy.

"A week away from home," said Mal uncertainly.

"A week of relaxation," said Jessi.

"A week of reading and lounging," I said. "I'm going to turn into the Leicester Lodge Lounge Lizard."

Everyone laughed. Then Dawn added, "A week of snow."

And Claudia said, "A week of junk-food opportunities. Remember those wonderful sweets machines on every floor?"

Dawn, our health-food addict, groaned. "I remember the salad bar in the dining hall."

"I'm getting nervous," Mal said suddenly.

"Me, too," agreed Jessi.

"What if we don't *like* the food?" asked Mallory.

"Or spending a week under our teachers' noses?" said Jessi.

"Forget it," answered Claud. "If you survived Camp Mohawk, you can survive any food. Anyhow, the teachers don't seem nearly as much like . . . teachers outside school. They just seem like

13

ordinary adults. After a while, they sort of blend into the woodwork and you hardly notice them."

"Really?" said Jessi and Mal at the same time.

"Really," the rest of us replied.

And at that moment, a huge cheer rose up in the car-park.

"The coaches are here!" someone shouted.

My friends and I turned to look. Goodbye, Connecticut, I thought. Hello, Vermont!

2nd CHAPTER

Stacey

Monday

Dear Laine,
Hi. If my writing looks funny, it's because I'm on a coach and the ride is bumpy. We (everyone in school) are on our way to Hooksett Crossing, Vermont, to that lodge I told you about. Can you believe that the population of Hooksett Crossing is only about 2,500? I worked out that there are more than three thousand times that many people in New York City.
Wish me luck in the winter war. I'm in the Blue Team. Also, keep your fingers crossed that we don't get snowed in up there.

Luv 'n' stuff,
Stacey

The coach trip to Vermont was amazing! Luckily I was prepared for it, having done it in seventh grade. I was also prepared for the goodbye scene with my mother at the school car-park. It wasn't as bad as I'd thought it would be. There were the usual tears (hers) and the reminders about how to take care of myself, as if I hadn't been doing it for several years already.

"Remember your insulin, darling," she said.

"I will, Mum."

"You did pack your injection kit, didn't you?" (I have to give myself insulin injections every day, in order to control my diabetes. The insulin keeps my blood sugar at a manageable level. If I forget the injections or forget to stick to my diet, my blood sugar goes out of control, and then I get really ill.)

"Yes, it's packed," I told Mum. "I never forget it."

"And you'll remind your teacher to remind the cook about your diet?"

"Yes." I was getting impatient. I could see my friends waiting in the car-park and I was dying to join them.

"Darling, I'm just checking," said Mum. "That's part of my job as a mother."

I smiled. Then I kissed Mum. She let me get out of the car, and I ran to my friends. I knew that after I met them, when I turned around, Mum would still be in the car-park, watching me. So I turned around and waved to her. She waved back. Then she drove off.

Free at last!

And now we were on the coach. My friends and I, all seven of us, had managed to get on the same coach. It was going to be a long trip to Hooksett Crossing. We weren't due to arrive there until the middle of the afternoon, weather permitting. But we weren't going to be on the coach *all* the time. The trip included two stops, one of which we'd had already. That was a break to freshen up at a motorway service station. Our next stop would be at another service station, where we would eat lunch. I was looking forward to that break.

But I was getting nervous about the weather. It had definitely looked like snow in Stoneybrook that morning. And the weather reports for Vermont included predictions for two snowstorms, one of which (a small one) was supposed to arrive late in the afternoon. The teachers were hoping it would arrive after we reached the lodge. The boys were hoping it would arrive before, so that we could have some excitement. The girls were divided. Half wanted excitement, the other half wanted to get to the lodge in time for dinner. (The food is pretty good up there, not like at Camp Mohawk.)

I felt someone tap me on the shoulder. It was Kristy, sitting behind me in a seat by herself.

17

"Stacey?" she said. "I've got a terrible problem."

"What is it?" I asked, alarmed.

"The theme from *Gilligan's Island* is running through my head and I can't get rid of it."

I couldn't help laughing. It didn't matter, since Kristy was laughing, too. Then she said, "I forget, Stace. Are you playing a rôle in the Winter Carnival?"

I shook my head. "No. But I plan to enter every contest in the war. Oh, except cross-country skiing. I've never been on cross-country skis before."

Kristy nodded. Her rôle in the carnival was going to be a huge one. Not only was she team captain, but she had volunteered to organize the *whole war*—to arrange every practice session and event, to encourage kids to compete (she'd never get Mary Anne), and to help keep score.

"I'm wondering if I made a mistake," said Claud, who was sitting next to me. (We were trying to ignore the group of boys in the back of the coach who were singing "I'm Henry the Eighth". Every time they got to the part that went, "Second verse same as the first, a little bit louder and a little bit worse" the *boys* got a little bit louder and a little bit worse. We were waiting for a teacher to notice this and yell at them.)

"A mistake?" I repeated.

Claud nodded. "By agreeing to judge the snow

sculpture contest instead of entering it. I really want to make a snow sculpture, but if I did, I couldn't be the judge. It'll be hard enough trying to judge without favouring the Red Team."

"I think you made the right choice," I told Claud. "The teachers really need you to be the judge." What I didn't say was that Claudia really needed the extra marks she'd earn for school.

"I suppose so," said Claud, not sounding at all sure of her decision.

Dawn, Mal, and I were the only club members without rôles in the Winter Carnival which would earn us extra marks. Mary Anne was going to be the historian, Kristy was going to run the war, Claud was going to judge the snow sculptures, and Jessi was in charge of Talent Night. That meant organizing a whole talent show, helping the kids with their acts, arranging rehearsals and more. This year was the first time the rôle had been given to a sixth-grader, but we all knew Jessi could handle it.

Then there were Dawn and Mal and I. Dawn and I simply hadn't found any rôles that interested us. Mal, on the other hand, had brought along a project of her own—her diary. I wasn't sure exactly what she planned to do with it, but she'd said it was going to keep her busy.

"Hey, Mary Anne," I said suddenly, leaning across the aisle.

"Yes?" Mary Anne was busy ducking. The

19

boys in the back were throwing crumpled chewing-gum wrappers all over the coach. The teachers, however, had noticed—finally—and had decided that the boys' restlessness meant that it was time to stop for lunch. Luckily the chosen service station was just a few kilometres away.

"How are you going to research the history of the lodge and the town?" I asked Mary Anne.

"Oh, the teachers said there's plenty of information in the lodge's library. Also, a lot of people who work at the lodge grew up in Hooksett Crossing, and some of them are quite old. They'll have information, too."

"That doesn't sound so bad," I said.

Mary Anne shook her head—and ducked again. And just then, the coach started to slow down. It rounded a corner and ahead of us, off to the right, I could see a large service station. Several school coaches (ours!) had already pulled into the car-park. We followed them and parked in a row. Then the coaches began to empty, and we SMS pupils (all 382 of us) trooped inside a building and into what must have been the world's largest cafeteria. Honestly, it looked just like our school cafeteria, only bigger. It wasn't the same place where we'd eaten lunch on last year's trip to the lodge.

"What I can't work out," I said to Claud as we stepped inside, "is why the people behind the counters look so horrified. You'd think they'd be glad to have our business. Besides, don't you suppose they're used to large groups of people? Their car-park is the size of Texas. So is their restaurant."

"Maybe they're not used to *this* big a group," replied Claud.

Anyway, what the frantic restaurant workers didn't know was that most of us had brought our own lunches and just needed places to sit down. We found them quickly. The room was full of tables, and soon the tables were full of us.

My friends and I grabbed a big round table for ourselves. We unpacked our lunches, began to eat—and for the next half hour were up and down in our seats like jack-in-the-boxes. First Kristy got paper napkins for us, then Mal decided she wanted a drink, then I decided the same thing,

then Jessi bought an orange, then Claud spotted a tray of crisps, and so on. It was the most unpeaceful meal imaginable. I was glad to get back on the coach, even knowing that the boys had plans to start singing "John Jacob Jingleheimer Schmidt".

As the kids in our school trooped out of the restaurant, every single worker let out a huge sigh of relief. It was as if the building went, "Whoosh" as we walked outside into the . . . snow!

Snow had started to fall while we were eating.

Several kids began to shout. Someone yelled, "Hooray! We're going to be snowbound at Leicester Lodge!"

"Really?" asked Jessi nervously as we BSC members boarded our coach.

"I doubt it," I replied, but I wasn't sure.

It had only been snowing for ten or fifteen minutes and already the ground was white. Although the time was 1:15 in the afternoon, the sky had begun to grow dark. We ran for our seats, everyone scrambling to sit next to the windows in order to watch the storm as closely as possible.

"Are we going to turn back?" Alan Gray shouted to the teachers. (The teachers were up near the front of the coach in a huddle.)

"No," one teacher replied. "We're much closer to Hooksett Crossing than to Stoneybrook."

So we drove slowly towards Leicester Lodge.

By three o'clock we were running very late.

The roads were treacherous. The wind and the snow were blowing hard and the drivers of the coaches (we tried to stick together—a convoy of SMS students) had to crawl along at a snail's pace. The coach was quiet as everyone strained to watch the road.

We were just ten miles from Hooksett Crossing when a deer leaped in front of our coach.

Immediately our driver slammed on the brakes. We missed the deer but we ran into a snowy embankment on the side of the road.

Everyone screamed. Claudia and I clutched hands.

By some miracle no one was hurt, and also the coach behind us stayed where it belonged—on the road. The driver of that coach pulled in front of us, parked, then got out to give our driver a hand in reversing out. Ten minutes later we were on the road again.

When someone on the silent coach finally said in a hushed voice, "Ooh, *there's* the lodge," I nearly cried, I was so relieved.

Claud looked at me. "We're here," she said.

"Yes," I replied. "Lodge sweet lodge."

3rd CHAPTER

Dawn

Monday

Dear Dad and Jeff,
        We really had an
adventure getting to Leicester
Lodge today! On the way to
Vermont a snowstorm hit us
and the driving got really
bad. Then a deer jumped
in front of the bus and our
driver ran into a snowbank.
No one was hurt, but were
we ever so scared. Some
kids started to cry, including
some boys. (Also Mary Anne,
who was sitting next to me.)
Don't worry. We got to the
lodge (which is huge) safe

Dawn

and sound, just late and nervous. Now the fun can begin!

Love and Sunshine,
Dawn

When we finally reached the lodge, darkness had fallen, and the lodge was all lit up. It was snow-covered, too, and looked just like a scene on a Christmas card—the flakes still falling, the silvery-dark sky, and the yellow glow of the lodge.

The people who run the lodge, Mr and Mrs George, were really nice to us. We had arrived late and they knew we'd been delayed by the storm. Then they heard about the accident. They were terribly sympathetic. Mrs George clucked all over us—teachers too—like a mother hen as we stepped inside the lodge. Then she began directing us to various dormitories.

Mal gasped. "Ohhh," I heard her say softly as she took her first look at the inside of Leicester Lodge.

I know why she drew her breath in like that. It's because, although the lodge looks big from the outside, you don't *feel* its vastness until you're inside. Have you ever seen that Stephen King film *The Shining*? Remember the Overlook Hotel, where all the scary things happened? Remember how big it was? Well, that's pretty much how the

25

lodge looks. I mean, it's just wing after wing, floor after floor, room after room. Most of the left end of the lodge is made up of dormitories (as opposed to rooms or suites), and that's where Mrs George took us.

"Three other groups will be here this week," she told us. "One is the eighth-graders from a junior high school in northern Vermont, another is the seventh- and eighth-graders from a middle school in New Hampshire, and we're still expecting a group of elementary school children from Maine."

Goody, I thought. I like meeting new people.

After walking for what seemed like miles, Mrs George and the teachers began directing large groups of us into various dormitories. Each room was so big it could sleep fifty-six people—two rows of fourteen bunk beds each.

"Bunk beds," moaned Stacey. "I'd forgotten. Just like at Camp Mohawk."

"No, *not* just like at Camp Mohawk," I replied. "At camp we didn't have chests of drawers or a rug on the floor or mirrors on the wall."

"Or en suite bathrooms," added Kristy.

"How am I ever going to find my way around?" wailed Mal as the BSC members, still in a group, continued to follow Mrs George down the hall.

"We'll have to leave a trail of breadcrumbs," said Jessi.

I glanced at Mary Anne and grinned. Then I

said, "No, you won't. Really. Last year was my first year here and I thought the same th—"

"Okay, the rest of the sixth-grade girls into this room," called Mr Bailey, an English teacher.

"They're grouping us by *grades*!" exclaimed Mal in dismay.

We'd been so busy talking we hadn't noticed.

"Did they break us up by grade last year?" I asked Mary Anne.

"I don't remember. I suppose so. Anyway, it didn't matter because the BSC members were all in the same grade," she replied.

We said a sad goodbye to Jessi and Mal (I really thought Mal was going to cry), then the last hundred or so of us continued down the hall. We stopped to separate the seventh-grade boys from the eighth-grade girls when we reached the boys' dormitory, and then we girls were shown into a final room. Our school filled seven dormitories altogether.

Mary Anne, Stacey, Claud, Kristy, and I went into our room.

"Hello, room!" said Kristy, who was getting silly.

"Our home for the next five days," I added.

It really was a very nice room, except for the bunks. But even the bunk beds were a lot nicer than the ones at camp, which looked as though someone had thrown some trees into the cabins and carved the beds out of them right there.

Dawn

A soft tan carpet covered the floor, and next to each set of bunks was a chest of drawers. Over the chest of drawers was a mirror, and—

"There're the bathrooms!" announced Kristy, pointing to the door at one end of the room.

A few girls dropped their bags and made a dash for the bathrooms. The rest of us scrambled to claim bunk beds. Mary Anne and I got a pair. (My mum is going out with Mary Anne's dad, and we thought that being bunk-mates would be good practice in case we ever ended up as stepsisters.) Next to us were Stacey and Claud. Poor Kristy was left without a bunk-mate and looked a bit sorry for herself.

Then she began to wonder if she would even need a bunk-mate. "Maybe there are only fifty-four or fifty-five of us," she said excitedly. "I could have a pair of bunks to myself. I could sleep on the top tonight, the bottom tomorrow night, the top the third night, the—"

"I don't have a bunk-mate, Kristy," said a voice from behind us.

Kristy turned around. There was Ashley Wyeth, a weird, arty friend of Claudia's. She doesn't have many good friends besides Claud.

"You don't?" said Kristy. She wanted to be polite, but she couldn't help looking crestfallen.

None of us was sure what to do until Claudia said tactfully, "Hey, why don't Stacey and I move along one pair, and then Kristy, you and

Ashley can be right between Dawn and Mary Anne, and Stacey and me."

"Okay." Kristy managed not to sound *too* reluctant. Then, brightening, she added, "Hey Ashley, can I have the top bunk?"

Ashley shrugged. "Of course."

Kristy didn't have to worry. Ashley would be a pushover to share with. Besides, how could Kristy lose, surrounded by all her friends?

"Come on, all of you, let's unpack," said Stacey. "Then we can go exploring. We don't have to be anywhere until six-thirty, when they serve dinner."

"Go exploring?" I repeated. "We already know where everything is."

"Yes, but Mal and Jessi don't. And they looked rather terrified when we left them. I thought we could give them a tour."

I smiled at Stacey. "Good idea."

So the five of us unpacked quickly. Then we got ready to find the sixth-grade girls' dormitory. Claud asked Ashley if she wanted to come with us, but Ashley was sprawled on the floor, sketching. She barely heard the question. We found our way to Mal and Jessi's room and were greeted by cries of, "You found us!" and, "We knew you'd come back!"

I couldn't help laughing. "You two are supposed to be having *fun*," I pointed out.

"How can we have fun when we don't even know where we are?" asked Mal.

"Look, I'll give you a hint," said Mary Anne. "Every floor is the same, except for the ground floor, so you can stop worrying about floors one to three. They're all rooms or dormitories. Just learn the way from your dormitory to the ground floor, okay?"

"Let's go all the way upstairs," said Claud as the seven of us walked into the hallway. "Then we'll work our way down and prove to them that the first, second and third floors are all the same."

We decided that was a good idea, and took the lift to the third floor.

"See?" I said when the doors opened. "This is just like our floor, the first floor."

"By the way, there's the third-floor, D-wing, sweets machine," added Claud.

We rode to the second floor. "There's the second-floor, D-wing sweets machine," said Claud.

We rode to the first floor. "There's *our* sweets machine," said Claud.

We rode to the ground floor. "There's the dining hall," said Claud as we got out of the lift.

"Home of Claudia's favourite salad bar," I added.

Claud scrunched up her nose and made a horrible face.

"Anyway," said Kristy to Jessi and Mal, "now

you know how to get from your dormitory to the dining hall."

"Do we have to go up and look at all the sweets machines each time?" asked Jessi, and the rest of us laughed.

"Now we'll show you the really good things," I said. "Follow this corridor in this direction and you come to . . . the common room. This is the main room of the lodge. The reception desk is here, but it's also a gathering area."

"Look at the fireplace!" said Jessi. "It's so big."

"This is a beautiful room," added Mal.

She was right. The common room was a long, lofty room with beams in the ceiling. It was built of brick and wood. Tables and chairs were grouped for playing board games or cards. There were big easy chairs for reading in. Under our feet was a woolly carpet. Kids and teachers were already drifting down from the dormitories. Some of the other guests were finding seats near the fire.

It was just when Jessi was suggesting that we continue the tour that the front door burst open, blowing snow on to the carpet, and two half-frozen people, a man and a woman, staggered inside. The man immediately collapsed on the ground.

"Oh, my lord!" cried Claudia.

A crowd of hotel workers rushed to help the people. Someone slammed the door shut. Everyone was asking questions. Finally the woman said, "You've got to help us. Please. We had an accident about five kilometres down the road. Our coach overturned. We—"

"Coach?" said Mrs George, making her way through the crowd. "You're not from Conway Cove Elementary School, are you?"

"Yes! We are!" said the woman. "You must be Mrs George." (Mrs George nodded.) "Anyway, I think all the children are okay," the woman went on, "but my arm is fractured—at least, I'm pretty sure it is—and Jim—"

"Jim is going to be fine," spoke up the man on the floor. "I just needed to warm up." He raised his head a little. Then, tentatively, he pulled himself into a sitting position. "See? I'm okay. But we have got to get some help back to the children. They're alone with the coach driver, and he's not in very good shape. He'll need an ambulance. His leg is broken—badly."

"How did you get here?" asked Mrs George.

"We walked," said the man.

"For five kilometres? In this weather?" Mrs George was amazed. And everyone looked outside at the storm, which was growing worse by the second. Then Mrs George said, "We'll call the police and the rescue services right away."

Mary Anne and I looked at each other, stunned.

4th CHAPTER

Kristy

Monday evening

Dear Mum, Watson, Nannie, Sam, Charlie,
David Michael, Emily, Andrew, and
Karen:

The Winter Carnival really got
off to an exciting start. There were two
bus accidents today. Tomorrow we hold
practices for the Winter War events, and
the war begins on Wednesday. This is
our schedule:

Wed.	Thurs.	Fri.
ice-skating	snowball fight	downhill skiing
snow sculpture		x-country skiing

LOVE YOU LOTS, Kristy

Talk about excitement! I was beginning to think that maybe we were having too much of it. When that teacher fell through the doorway to the lodge, I thought I'd faint. And then the other teacher started talking about the children and the accident.

I have to say that the Georges remained calm and took charge of things very well. While Mr George phoned the police and the rescue services, Mrs George helped the teachers on to a sofa and phoned the hotel doctor.

"We have to drive back to the accident," the woman teacher was saying.

"Oh, no," said Mrs George. "Not you. Not either of you. But I'll get my husband to start our

coach and he and I and a couple of other teachers —we've got plenty here—" she added with a smile, "can go back to the accident and meet the ambulance. Then we'll bring the children here."

While Mrs George was talking, my brain was clicking along. I was getting an idea.

"Do we have any volunteers to brave the storm?" Mrs George asked the crowd that had gathered. "Teachers would be best, I think."

Before anyone could answer, I stepped forward and opened my big mouth. "We'll go," I said. "The Babysitters Club will go."

"The . . . what?" Mrs George looked flustered for the first time.

"The Babysitters Club. Us," I said simply, gesturing to my friends.

My maths teacher stepped forward. "They're good with children," he said. "They'd probably be a good choice." (We're very well known.)

Mrs George looked at the seven of us. "Well . . . terrific," she said finally. "I think some adults should go along too, though."

In the end, the Georges, three SMS teachers, and my friends and I were the ones who helped rescue the children. We scrambled into our warmest clothes and then piled on to the old school coach that was waiting in front of the lodge. Mr George was behind the steering wheel.

"We bought this coach eight years ago," Mrs

George told us. "Our son thought we were crazy, but it's come in handy more than once."

The coach pulled on to the road and drove slowly in the direction of the accident. Mrs George gave us some instructions. Then everyone on board grew silent. I tried to read the expressions on the faces of my friends, but it was too dark to see. I knew the club members were nervous but in control. Not one of them minded that I had volunteered our services. Children come first where we're concerned, and we've handled quite a few emergencies, as well as large groups of children. This was something we *had* to do.

The coach drove slowly along. Mr George wouldn't go faster than fifteen miles an hour because he didn't want us to crash, too. At long last I saw flashing red lights ahead.

"Look!" I said softly, nudging Dawn.

"Oh, wow!" Dawn strained forward to see what was going on.

Mr George drew the coach to a slow halt. Then he said, "Okay, everyone out. Help in any manner you think necessary, but don't get in the way of the rescue workers."

We piled out of the coach and surveyed the scene. The police and rescue services were already there. An ambulance, a tow truck, and three police cars were parked by the side of the road. Floodlights had been set up around the coach, so

37

we had a pretty good look at the accident itself. The coach seemed to have skidded off the road and down a short embankment before rolling over on to its side.

We arrived just as the ambulance men were struggling up the embankment, carrying a stretcher with the coach driver on it. Huddled around the coach were the children. There were sixteen of them. And every single one of them was crying. A police officer was trying to calm them, but she wasn't having much luck.

"Okay, you lot," I said to the other members of the BSC. "There are sixteen children and seven of us. Let's each take two or three and try to quieten them down, okay?"

"Okay," said Dawn, Jessi, Mal, Mary Anne, Stacey, and Claud in one voice.

We trudged down the embankment, holding hands when we needed to. The ground was incredibly slippery and the wind was howling and blowing snow in our faces so that it was difficult to see.

When we reached the children we didn't waste a second. I took the first two I saw and separated them from the others. (The police officer looked relieved.)

I had grabbed a boy and a girl. The boy was about eight and the girl perhaps seven. Neither one was wearing a hat, and the boy was missing a glove.

"Hello," I said to them. I squatted down in the snow so I was closer to their height. "My name is Kristy. Guess what. I'm staying at the lodge. The same place where you're going. You had a frightening accident, didn't you?"

"It was awful," wailed the girl.

"The coach driver is *dead*," added the boy.

"No, he isn't," I assured them. "He looked pretty bad, but your teacher said he's just broken his leg. Honestly. Now listen, it's freezing out here. Where are your hats? And where's your other glove?" I asked the boy. I took his bare hand in my mittens and rubbed it briskly.

"They came off when the coach fell over," said the boy. "Pinky even lost her shoe."

"Pinky? Who's Pinky?" I said. The children seemed calmer and I was glad.

"Pinky's that girl over there," answered the boy, pointing.

I looked around and saw that Stacey was carrying one of her children in order to keep her shoeless foot out of the snow. She was trying to warm the foot by wrapping it in someone's knitted hat.

"Oh," I said. "Listen, what are your names? I told you mine, but I don't know yours."

"I'm Bryce," said the boy.

"I'm Ginnie," said the girl.

"Okay, Bryce and Ginnie. Bryce, you keep your bare hand in your pocket, all right?"

39

Bryce nodded.

"Now, listen," I went on. "Is either one of you hurt? Do you hurt anywhere?"

The children shook their heads.

"Are you sure?"

"Yes," said Ginnie. Then she asked in a wavery voice, her eyes starting to fill with tears again, "What's going to happen now?"

Mrs George had explained that to us on the way to the scene of the accident. With the nearest hospital almost fifty kilometres away, we were just going to take the children back to the lodge and let the doctor there examine them, unless any of them looked seriously injured or had been knocked unconscious or something. Luckily, all the children seemed to be fine, just cold and scared.

"We're going to drive back to the lodge and get you warmed up," I said. "There's a big fire burning in the fireplace, and it's almost suppertime. Oh, and I know a secret about the cook at Leicester Lodge."

"What?" said Bryce and Ginnie eagerly.

"He makes the *best* hot chocolate in the *world*," I whispered.

"Really?" asked Ginnie, intrigued.

"Really."

By this time most of the children had stopped crying, and the teachers had gathered up all the loose things—hats and shoes and gloves and lunch boxes—from the crash site that they could

40

find. Now a police officer had managed to climb inside the crippled coach and was handing suitcases through the windows to the Georges.

Very quickly, the teachers, the children, their equipment, and we BSC members were back on the Georges' coach, the heater going full blast.

Before we left, Mrs George pulled something out of her pocket. It turned out to be a list of all the children who were supposed to be on the bus. The teacher with the fractured arm had given it to her. Mrs George took a roll call and two head counts before she'd let her husband start up the coach.

Good thinking, I decided.

The teachers were sitting in the back of the coach with the children's suitcases and armloads of loose things they'd found in the snow. It's amazing how much stuff sixteen children can get on a coach for a simple five-day holiday.

My friends and I and the children were sitting closer to the front. We were crowded three or four across in the seats. We could have spread out more, but the children were so frightened that they'd become clingy and wouldn't let us out of their sight. Some of them wouldn't even let go of our hands.

As we ploughed slowly through the snow back to the lodge, Mary Anne spoke up. "Listen, everyone."

"Yes?" we said.

"Could you do me a favour? You know the book I'm making for Logan?"

"Yes?" we said again.

"Well, considering what's just happened, I have a feeling this is going to be an . . . unusual week. I want Logan to know what *really* goes on. I mean, not just from my point of view. So do you think you could each make a few notes every day? Just jot down things that happen—to you or to anyone else. Whatever you think is important."

"Of course," the rest of us replied.

"Oh, good," said Mary Anne. "Then I'll collect your notes at the end of each day and try to put everything together so that Logan has a—" Mary Anne stopped talking. She pointed to me and I looked down at my sides.

Bryce and Ginnie were sound asleep. They were leaning heavily against me. The other children were falling asleep, too. My friends and I stopped talking. We rode to the lodge in silence.

5th CHAPTER

Claudia

monday nigt

Hi, mary anne these are my notes four you.

Well I have never seen little childern wake up so fast. One minut they were sleeping on the coches the next minut they were in the loge and wide awake. First the loge docter checked the kids. Then we ate dinner. We were all streving After that we had to ~~wrok~~ work (stacey helped me spell that) ont waht to do whith the kids since there teachers were at the hospitle....

Everything happened awfully quickly after we reached the lodge again (safely, I might add). As we pulled up at the front door, Kristy said softly, "Wake up, everyone. We're here."

Well, those children looked up sleepily—and then they came to life! They tore off the bus, and through the front door, which Mrs George held open for them. Then Ginnie, the little girl who Kristy had talked to, came to a screeching halt and began yelling, "Miss Weber! Mr Dougherty! Where are you?"

Of course, a crowd gathered. Everyone wanted to see "the poor little children who'd been in the horrible bus accident". (I actually heard one woman say that.) Luckily Mr George appeared around the same time that my friends and I caught up with the children.

Mr George told them straightforwardly that Miss Weber and Mr Dougherty, the two teachers who had braved the snow, had been taken to hospital for a check-up, but that they'd only be there overnight.

"What about us?" wailed Joey, one of the children I was looking after.

Good question. I looked at the Georges. They were looking at each other. Finally Mrs George said, "First the doctor wants to examine you. Then I think we should eat dinner. It was served over an hour ago. I'm hungry. How about you?"

We were starved, which is not good for Stacey.

With her diabetes, she shouldn't skip meals. It messes up her blood sugar or something. The children were hungry, too, after their adventure. So after the doctor had given them a clean bill of health, everyone from the coach went into the dining hall. We sat at two of the long tables. The BSC members scattered themselves among the children, in order to give them a hand if they needed it. When the food came we *gobbled* it down. That's how hungry we were. And since, unlike the cooks at camp, the head cook here is nice and really listens to people, there was no food served (except dessert) that Stacey couldn't eat. (The Camp Mohawk cook kept serving sugary stuff, like salads with honey dressing, that Stacey's not allowed to eat.)

Anyway, when dinner was over, Mrs George turned the sixteen children over to the cook, who took them into the kitchen to show them how he and his helpers prepare food for hundreds of people every day. As soon as they were gone, Mrs George said to the rest of us, who were still sitting at the dining tables, "I want to thank you so much for your help tonight. You don't *know* how my husband and I appreciate it. Lots of groups of school children visit the lodge each winter, but nothing like this has ever happened."

"I hate to bring this up," said Mr Cheney, one of the SMS teachers, "but what about the children? What are they going to do now?"

Mrs George sat down. "I'm not sure," she said. "They'll stay here tonight, of course. We can't send them back to Maine in this weather, particularly not without their teachers. But I suppose they could go back tomorrow. I hate to deprive them of this trip, though. They won it."

"They won it?" I repeated.

Mrs George nodded. "Their school sponsored a readathon. These are the winners. They worked hard and they've really been looking forward to this. They come from a small town and most of their families don't have much money. This is the first time some of them have been away from Conway Cove. We'll have to ring their parents tonight to tell them what happened. I'm sure the children will want to talk to them anyway. Maybe after a few phone calls we'll have a better idea of what to do with the children. The school might be able to send down some parents to act as chaperones or something. Thank goodness none of the children are hurt. They could easily stay here if we can just find someone to keep an eye on them."

"What about the teachers who went to the hospital?" said Mr Cheney. "Won't they be back tomorrow?"

Mr George answered that question. "Yes, but they'll be out of action, at least for any activities such as skiing or skating. As you know, Miss Weber broke her arm. And the doctor here at the lodge thought Mr Dougherty might have cracked several ribs."

At this point I nudged Kristy.

"What?" she said. She'd been deep in thought.

"We could help," I whispered. "We could look after the children."

Kristy smiled. "Exactly what I was thinking. Should I say something?"

"Nothing ever stopped you before."

Ooh. If looks could kill . . . . But Kristy tried to forget what I'd said. She stood up slowly.

"Excuse me," she said. "I have an idea." She glanced from Stacey to Jessi to Mal to Dawn to Mary Anne, silently asking their permission to volunteer our services. My friends nodded. "Well," Kristy went on, "my friends and I could take care of the children this week."

"We could even share rooms with them," I added. "We could just move our things into another dormitory and share with the children."

"Well, that would be wonderful," replied Mrs George, "but I don't know. It's up to your teachers."

"I don't know, either," said Mr Cheney, and I felt myself deflate like a balloon with a hole in it. "Do you girls really want to give up your holiday?" he asked.

"I don't think we'd be giving it up," said Kristy. "If Miss Weber and Mr Dougherty can help watch the children while they're indoors, we can just include them in our regular activities. We'll take turns doing special things with them. We won't mind. The children can even come to our talent show."

"Or be *in* it!" said Jessi excitedly.

"We're used to children, believe me," added Kristy.

"You're sure this is something you *want* to do?" asked Mr Cheney. "It's not playtime, you know. It's a big responsibility—and it's for five days."

"We know and we're sure," said Kristy firmly.

"Right," we agreed.

"The lodge would be glad to pay you for your help," spoke up Mrs George.

That time, Kristy didn't even need to look at the rest of us for our opinions. "Thanks," she replied, "but that's okay. We don't need to be paid. We're still going to have a great time here. Besides, every year, you and Mr George let our whole school come here and I know we never pay you enough for it. The least we can do is help some of the other children you're giving a treat to."

Well, Kristy should know better than to say something like that to an adult. Of course Mrs George began to cry because she was so touched. We BSC members decided it was time to leave. Besides, the cook was bringing the children back.

When Mrs George recovered, she showed us to an empty dormitory. While my friends and I gathered our possessions and moved them into the children's room, Mrs George and the children phoned their parents, and the SMS teachers carried the children's belongings to the room. As soon as they left, we decided to get them ready for bed. First, though, we had to sort out that mountain of woolly hats and mittens and things. We spent nearly half an hour holding up one item at a time, saying, "Whose is this?" and waiting for someone to call out, "Mine!"

When everything was finally organized, Kristy said, "Okay, everyone, change into your pyjamas."

I've never heard such screaming in my life. Uh-oh—we were in a mixed dormitory. The boys wouldn't change in front of the girls and the girls

wouldn't change in front of the boys. And neither group trusted the other to close their eyes or turn their backs. Finally we worked out an arrangement. Since there were fewer boys, they could change in the bathroom, while we girls changed in the dormitory. The boys had to promise not to come out of the bathroom until we said it was okay. Even so, the girls changed clothes as if they were on fire.

At long last, each of our charges was tucked up in bed.

Ahhh, I thought as my friends and I climbed wearily into *our* beds. No sooner were the covers pulled up and the lights turned off than a little voice said, "Stacey? My foot hurts. It didn't hurt before, but now it does."

It was Pinky. Stacey got out of bed and looked at Pinky's foot. She thought it seemed swollen so she called the lodge doctor, who arrived at once, examined Pinky's foot, pronounced her ankle slightly sprained (undoubtedly as a result of the crash), bandaged it, and told her to stay off it the next day. Then he quickly looked at the other children again and found them fine but sleepy.

When he left, I turned off the lights for a second time. "Goodnight, everybody," I said.

" 'Night, Claudia," said a chorus of voices. Then all the children began saying goodnight to each other, one at a time. That was an awful lot of "goodnights", but my friends and I let them do it because we knew they were still nervous and frightened.

It was eleven o'clock before the last of us fell asleep.

6th CHAPTER

Mary Anne

Tuesday

When we woke up the next morning, the snow was still falling. It was funny, Logan. I should have been excited about the day that lay ahead, but I couldn't work up any enthusiasm. All I could think about was you and Aruba and whatever you were doing down there. I suppose there are a lot of beautiful girls on an island like that.

To take my mind off those thoughts, I concentrated on the sixteen children my friends and I were caring

for. Their parents had
given them permission to
stay at the lodge as planned,
so now they really were
our charges. (Teachers don't
share with pupils. They
have their own rooms.)
I wondered what the day
would bring.

I woke very slowly and groggily the next morning. It's amazing how much a few out-of-the-ordinary events can drain you. I realized I was still tired, even though we'd had plenty of sleep the night before.

I peered around our semi-dark room. Mrs George had put us in a small, oddly shaped dormitory. There were just twelve bunks in it. Dawn and I were sharing again, so were Jessi and Mal, and so were Stacey and Claud. Kristy had thought she had another chance for a bunk all to herself since there was an uneven number of us, but no such luck. Apparently, none of the children wanted to share with Pinky, so Pinky ended up alone, and Kristy shared with Ginnie, who seemed pretty attached to her.

Around me the children were still sound asleep. I glanced at Claudia, Kristy, and Stacey. They were dead to the world. I leaned over the side of my bed and peered down at Dawn. She was snoring.

Mary Anne

It should have been a happy morning. Outside, the snow was still falling—heavily. I *love* snow, but for some reason I couldn't work up any enthusiasm about it. I knew that downstairs the cooks were preparing a big, yummy breakfast, and I was hungry, but I couldn't work up any enthusiasm about breakfast, either. Worse still, I was pretty sure the children would wake up in good spirits, since they'd been fairly perky by bedtime the night before, and *very* excited about the prospect of skiing and skating that day.

But I just didn't feel . . . I don't know. Something was nagging at me. I couldn't put my finger on it.

I looked at my watch. It was seven-thirty. Breakfast would be served at eight. I climbed out of bed, wishing that I'd got the bottom bunk instead of the top, but Dawn had claimed the bottom right away—in both our old dormitory and the one we'd moved into the night before.

I turned on the lights in the room.

All around me I heard moaning and groaning.

"How can it be morning already?" mumbled Claud.

"I could sleep forever," added Jessi.

"Me, too," echoed Mal. "Forever and *ever*."

"It's still snowing," I announced, trying to sound cheerful. "Look outside. It's a fairyland. All you can see is white."

Kristy was the only one who looked outside.

"*Oh,*" she said, sounding incredibly depressed. "If this keeps up, we won't be able to hold practices today. What a bore. The events start tomorrow. We *have* to practise."

"Calm down," said Dawn. "People are always skiing when it's snowing. And I'm sure someone from the lodge will clear the skating pond."

"I suppose so," Kristy replied distractedly.

"Well, come *on*, everybody," I said loudly. "Up you get. Twenty minutes until breakfast."

Our sleepy charges aroused themselves slowly. The boys looked like zombies as they headed for the bathroom. But the girls came to life quickly and dressed in record time, afraid that the boys would come out of the bathroom before we'd given them the all-clear.

The children were dressed and making their beds when someone knocked on our door.

"Come in!" called Kristy.

And into our room stepped . . . dum da-dum dum . . . Miss Halliday—my least favourite teacher at SMS. She teaches seventh-grade girls' gym, and last year she'd been the bane of my existence. I couldn't stand her and she couldn't stand me. That's because Miss Halliday doesn't like hopeless cases. And I'm hopeless. I'm no good at sports, which is why I wasn't taking part in the Winter War.

As you can probably imagine, though, Kristy and Miss Halliday get along extremely well. Gym

55

instructors don't usually have teachers' pets, but Miss Halliday was an exception. Her pet had been Kristy, the great athlete of the world, and they were still friends this year, even though Miss Halliday was no longer Kristy's teacher.

Anyway, when she poked her head into our room, I just froze. It was like the beginning of another dreaded volleyball game. I could almost hear her saying, "Okay, Mary Anne, *serve* . . . . No, *over* the net. Use a little power. Put some muscle into it."

But of course that was not what Miss Halliday said. Instead, she said, "In all the confusion last night, I forgot to tell you that I'm one of your dormitory supervisors. The others will be Miss Weber and Mr Dougherty, as soon as they get back from hospital. The three of us will help you with the Conway Cove pupils. That's what we're here for, okay? I can give them a hand with outdoor activities and the others can oversee indoor activities. That way, you members of the Babysitters Club will be able to have some time to yourselves."

"Thanks, Miss Halliday!" exclaimed Kristy.

Miss Halliday left then and my friends and I helped the children with last-minute chores— shoe-tying, hair-plaiting, etc. I did everything mechanically, like a robot who has been programmed to perform. When we were ready, we left our dormitory and Kristy showed the children the way downstairs to the dining hall. (Claudia showed them the sweets machine.)

The twenty-three of us filed into breakfast and chose a table to ourselves. We ate hungrily — scrambled eggs, toast, and fruit. And after that, we were on our own. It was snowing less heavily and Kristy announced skiing practice for the morning. The Conway Cove children were eager to try skiing, so Miss Halliday bundled them up (except for Pinky) and took them off to one of the beginners' lessons.

By ten o'clock in the morning, I found myself more or less on my own. Kristy, Claud, Dawn, and Stacey were skiing, Mallory was off doing something with her secret diary project, and Jessi had volunteered to entertain Pinky for the day, since Pinky was under doctor's orders to stay inside with her foot up. If the pain and swelling in her ankle had gone by the evening, then she would be able to do whatever she wanted the next day.

What should I do with myself? I wondered. Even though I didn't really feel like working, I decided I might as well get on with my job as historian for the Winter Carnival. There were only four days in which to do my research. Once I got back to Stoneybrook, I had to be ready to write up the project. I certainly wasn't going to be able to do any research on tiny Hooksett Crossing or on Leicester Lodge anywhere but here.

Mary Anne

So I went upstairs to our dormitory, found a pad of paper and a pen, and went back downstairs to the room next to the common room. It was the Leicester Lodge library.

The books in the library are there for the guests to read and enjoy. Most of them are novels, mysteries, and skiing guides, but on a shelf near a ceiling-to-floor window, I found two rows of books on local history. I looked at a few of the titles: *A Brief History of Hookset Crossing, Rutledge County: A Retrospective, Ski Resorts in Vermont.* There were quite a few more, too. Most of them were written by local authors and published by small Vermont printers. Then one title caught my eye: *Leicester Lodge: 1920 to 1980*, by Thomas George. Thomas George . . . could that be Mr George? I checked the book jacket. It was! His picture was there and everything.

Well. The teachers had been right. There was plenty of information for my report. I pulled several books off the shelf, piled them up on an end table, and curled up in an armchair to start taking a few notes. Most of the books covered boring things like population statistics, agricultural information, weather and weather patterns, as well as a lot about how to make maple syrup. But nearly every book mentioned one chilling story: the tale of the ghost of Leicester Lodge.

My heart began to pound. I hadn't heard about any ghost before. Why hadn't last year's historian

58

uncovered this information? Then I remembered. There hadn't been a historian the year before. No one had volunteered for the job. No one had volunteered when I was in sixth grade, either. It took a twit like me to volunteer. No wonder the teachers had been so thrilled when I'd put up my hand.

I shivered. The ghost of Leicester Lodge. Did Mr George mention it in his book? He certainly did. He devoted three chapters to it, finally concluding that there was no ghost—there were just a lot of people with big imaginations.

Immediately, I ran to the kitchen to interview the cook and some of the hotel workers.

"Is there a ghost at the lodge?" I asked the cook breathlessly.

"Some say so," he replied cryptically.

"Well, have you ever seen it?"

"Might have."

"What do you mean?"

"Just what I said. Maybe I have, and maybe I haven't."

I gave up with the cook. I asked a couple of the kitchen assistants about the ghost. Then asked two of the housekeepers. I got the same sorts of answers from everyone.

Hmmm. What a puzzle. This was really interesting. Everyone seemed to be covering up when it came to the ghost story. I moved my pile of books from the library to the common room. I now really did have something to write about! I opened my notebook at a clean page, and after much thought I wrote:

My dearest Logan,

You can't possibly know how much I miss you. My thoughts are with you and only you every second of every day. During the night, you fill my dreams. I cannot bear to be apart from you.

I paused in my writing. I was picturing Logan on a beach in Aruba, lying on a towel next to some gorgeous girl—a girl who wasn't shy and who was good in gym. With great difficulty, I managed to finish the letter. It was six pages long. The entire last page consisted of xxx's. I wondered if it would reach Aruba before the Brunos left, decided that it wouldn't, and didn't post it.

I also didn't write a word of my history project.

7th CHAPTER

Jessi

Tuesday

Today went a little differently than I'd thought it would. Right up until this morning, I'd been pretty sure I'd spend it learning to ski or practising my skating. Instead, I ended up watching Pinky Winkler. To be honest, I didn't exactly end up watching her. I sort of volunteered for the job....

Jessi

When I woke up this morning, I was so excited . . . once I got over the shock of actually waking up, that is. We (the BSC members and the Conway Cove children) were still pretty tired from the excitement of the night before. But when I looked out of the window and saw the snow, and later when I walked into the dining hall and smelled the toast and eggs and other good breakfast smells, I felt my energy return.

Kristy sat at our table, talking a mile a minute about the activities for the day: "Since it's still snowing, we'll have ski practice first," she said. "That'll give the lodge people time to clear the snow off the pond. We'll go skating in the afternoon if we can."

"Can *we* learn to ski?" asked Amber, one of the youngest children.

"Of course. There's a snowbunny trail especially for you, and a really nice instructor who'll show you what to do. And Miss Halliday will help you."

"Ooh, I can't wait!" exclaimed Ginnie. "I have never, ever been skiing."

"I went once," spoke up Joey. Joey had long straight brown hair with a fringe. His bottom middle teeth were missing, and so was a side one on top. "It was fun. But I fell down a lot."

Kristy grinned. Then she looked around at us BSC members. "Who else is coming to practise?" she asked.

63

"Me," said Stacey and Claudia at once.

"I'll come," added Dawn.

Kristy looked at Mary Anne.

"*Me?*" squeaked Mary Anne. "You must be joking!"

"Mal?" said Kristy.

Mallory shook her head. "I'm no good on skis. I'll be in the snowball fight, though, and Jessi and I have a good idea for a snow sculpture."

"Great," said Kristy. She turned to me. "Jessi? Skiing?"

I was just about to say, "Of course. Why not? I'd like to learn." But something stopped me. It was the image of myself dancing on stage. First I saw myself in *Coppélia*, then in *Swan Lake*. I saw myself whirling around and around and . . . falling! A huge plaster cast was on my leg and I was completely off balance.

How could I have been so stupid? I thought. I can't go skiing. I'm a dancer. I could break an arm or leg. Come to think of it, I couldn't very well go skating, either. What if I broke an ankle? Suddenly even the snowball fight didn't seem too safe. Suppose I got frostbitten and had to have my toes removed? I couldn't dance without my toes. I need them for balance.

"Um," I said, playing for time. "Um, I think I'll skip ski practice. Someone has to . . . has to watch Pinky. Yes, that's it. Because Miss Weber and Mr Dougherty aren't back from hospital yet."

"Oh, I can watch her," Mary Anne told me. "I'm just going to stay inside and work on my project."

"No, no, no," I said quickly. "That's okay. You'll need to concentrate, I'd better stay with Pinky. We'll have lots of fun, won't we, Pinky?"

"It'll be great," said Pinky dispiritedly.

I cringed slightly, remembering that none of the little children had wanted Pinky for their bunk-mate. What was wrong with her? I wondered. Oh, well, I couldn't worry about that. I needed an excuse, and Pinky was a good one.

"Well . . . okay," said Kristy. She pushed her plate away. "Come on, everyone. Let's get going!"

Kids and teachers were starting to file out of the dining hall, so we followed them. Mal and I walked on either side of Pinky, acting as crutches so that she could keep her injured foot off the ground. When we got to the common room, Mal said, "I'd better go. I'm working on my special project today."

"Oh, all right," I replied, suddenly dismayed at having volunteered to entertain Pinky until Miss Weber and Mr Dougherty returned.

Pinky and I sat on opposite sides of a game table. Pinky's foot stretched out on a chair.

We looked at each other.

"I'm Jessi," I said, just in case Pinky hadn't learned all our names yet.

"I know."

"Is Pinky your real name," I asked her, "or a nickname?"

Pinky made a face. "Of course it's a nickname," she replied. "What did you think? My parents wouldn't be stupid enough to give me a name like Pinky."

Gosh! I was just trying to make conversation. "What's your real name then?" I asked.

"Priscilla."

"I like Pinky better," I told her.

"I don't."

Yes, she really was unfriendly. No wonder none of the other children had wanted her for a bunk-mate.

"So how many books did you read in the readathon at your school?" I asked.

"Why do you want to know?"

"I'm *curious*," I answered, trying not to lose my temper.

Pinky sighed deeply. "Sixty-two."

"Gosh! That must be a record. You must really like to read."

"Duh."

I had no answer for "duh", so I kept my mouth shut.

"You know what I *don't* like?" said Pinky. "I don't like nosy people who ask lots of questions. So stop asking so many questions. In fact, stop talking to me."

Stop talking to her? Now who did that remind me of? Oh, yes. The woman who lives opposite us in Stoneybrook. She won't let her daughter, who's only a little younger than my sister, Becca, talk to me or Becca or anyone in our family — because we're black. She's even threatened to move out of her house, saying that a black family in the neighbourhood makes the property values of all the houses go down. She says she'll have to sell quickly before her house is worthless.

I hope she leaves soon.

I eyed Pinky across the table. Was she prejudiced, too? Would she talk like this to Mal or to Kristy? I wasn't sure. What I did know was that it was my job to entertain her, and I planned to do just that. Even if it meant talking to her.

"Well," I said, getting to my feet. "I feel like a game of Candy Land or maybe Scrabble."

"Do you know how to play poker?" asked Pinky.

"No. Sorry."

"Oh. I thought you would."

"Well, I don't. How about Scrabble?"

"All right. If we have to."

"We don't have to do anything. But doing *some*thing is better than sitting around all day."

Pinky sighed. "Okay. Let's play." She sounded as if I'd suggested scrubbing floors instead of playing a game.

The Georges keep a big collection of board games and packs of cards in a cupboard near the reception desk. Mary Anne had shown me where it was before she began her history research in the library. (She had also shown me the library.) I opened the cupboard and found Scrabble, Monopoly, Sorry, Snakes and Ladders, Memory, Risk and a lot of other games. I chose Scrabble and Memory, closed the cupboard, and went back to Pinky.

"Took you long enough," Pinky greeted me.

I almost said something really nasty to her, but I held my tongue. Insulting a person never helps a bad situation. Besides, Pinky's foot hurt her, and she'd had a bad scare the day before. I needed to keep things in perspective.

So all I said was, "Look. I brought two games. Have you ever played Memory?"

Pinky studied the box the game came in. "No," she replied.

"Which shall we play first?"

Pinky shrugged.

"Okay, if you don't care, then I'll choose," I said. "Let's play Memory."

"First get me a drink," said Pinky.

"A drink? We've just finished breakfast."

"I *know*. I'm thirsty anyway. Get me a drink."

What was I—Pinky's maid? To keep her quiet, I got her a drink from a machine.

She never thanked me.

We played three games of Memory. I won every round. I've got a very good memory.

But . . . "Cheat!" cried Pinky after the third round. "Dirty cheat!" She threw the cards back in the box.

Well, I didn't have to sit there while Pinky called me names and ordered me around. I could keep an eye on her from a distance. I got up, marched into the library, almost bumping into Mary Anne, who was leaving with an armload of books, pulled *Matilda*, by Roald Dahl, off the shelf of children's books, went back to the common room, and thrust the book into Pinky's hands.

69

Jessi

"Here," I said. "If you like to read so much, read this."

Then I sat down next to Mary Anne, who had settled herself near the fire with her books. But I got up again straight away. Mary Anne was looking really soppy. She was doodling her name and Logan's all over a piece of paper.

So I borrowed a piece of paper and a pencil from her and chose another seat from where I could keep an eye on Pinky. Then I began thinking up ideas for Talent Night. All morning I worked and Pinky read.

We didn't speak again till lunchtime.

8th CHAPTER

Stacey

Tuesday morning

What a morning! Here's something for your book, Mary Anne. I met the world's cutest guy today. His name is Pierre. Pierre D'Amboise. His family is French, but Pierre was born in the U.S and has lived here all his life. He doesn't speak with an accent. In fact, he admitted that he doesn't even speak much French. Pierre has deep, deep brown eyes that twinkle. I mean, they're really sparkly. And his voice is starting to change, which is so cool....

I could have gone on about Pierre for pages and pages, but I didn't think Mary Anne needed quite such detailed information. Besides, some of my thoughts about Pierre were personal. But before I start talking about him again, let me go back and tell you about the morning so I can explain how Pierre and I met.

It was still snowing when we woke up, and the first thing Mallory said was, "Do you really think we might get snowed—"

"Shh!" I hissed. I held my hand out to indicate that the children might overhear us. We didn't want to scare them all over again.

"Sorry," whispered Mal.

I looked outside at the snow. I happen to love snow. We didn't get all that much of it when I lived in New York City. My personal theory is that the city is too warm for snow. It's warm from body heat—millions of people live there. And the pavements and streets are warm because so much goes on underneath them—subways, underground shops and banks. That sort of thing.

There's very little chance of a blizzard in New York City.

I was almost hoping to get snowed in at Leicester Lodge. We'd have plenty of food and supplies, so we wouldn't be in any danger. However, I kept that thought to myself. I didn't think anyone else wanted to get snowed in.

At breakfast, Kristy announced ski practice for

the morning. The snow was already letting up a little, so there was really no reason not to go out.

"Are you coming with us?" Dawn asked as she and Kristy and Claudia were getting ready for a morning on skis.

"I'd like to, but I'd better not," I replied. "You're too good for me. I'll have to stay on the nursery slopes, at least at first. I offered to help Miss Halliday keep an eye on the children. I'm not going to have a lesson like the children are, but I think I'd better look in on their class from time to time. Fifteen children who've hardly ever been on skis are a lot for one teacher and one instructor to handle."

"Okay," said Kristy. "Practise hard, though. The Blue Team will need you on Friday."

"Yes, General," I replied.

Everyone laughed except Kristy.

I watched Dawn, Claud, and Kristy set off downstairs. Claudia, lugging her ski equipment. Then I watched Mal pull her diary from under her mattress (who was she fooling?) and leave the room with it, and I watched Mary Anne find a notepad and a pencil and leave with *them*. Pinky and Jessi had stayed downstairs, I knew. So it was just me, Miss Halliday, and fifteen children who needed to dress for snowy weather.

Honestly, I've never seen so many clothes. Each child wanted to put on (over his indoor clothes) a sweater, an extra pair of socks, plastic

73

bags over the sock layers to keep his feet dry inside the ski boots, two pairs of mittens, a hat, a scarf, and a snowsuit (and snowsuits are complicated things—zips, buttons, buckles, and press-studs everywhere).

It took us over half an hour to get those children dressed, and wouldn't you know it, no sooner did we think we'd finished than we started hearing things like:

"Stacey? I've got to go to the toilet."

"Me, too."

"Me, too."

"Stacey, I put my snowsuit on, but I forgot my sweater."

"Me, too."

"Bryce, stop it, you idiot!" (That was Joey. I'm not sure what he and Bryce were arguing about.)

"Stacey, my mittens don't match."

"Neither do mine."

After another fifteen or twenty minutes we were ready to go.

Sort of.

Have you ever tried to sort out skis, boots, and poles for fifteen children?

Probably not. I hadn't.

I expect you can imagine, though, that it took nearly forever, and I'm not exaggerating. By the time the children were *finally* ready, and Miss Halliday and I had our skis too, I couldn't wait for a run down one of the nursery slopes. But I knew I

74

ought to help the children get organized in their class, even though Miss Halliday kept saying, "Go on, Stacey. I've got things under control."

At last I took her advice. I took the ski lift to the top of one of the nursery slopes. A baby slope, Kristy would call it, but I prefer to say "nursery slope".

I managed to get off the lift without falling, to turn round, and to start off slowly down the slope. I tried to remember the few things I'd learned from the lessons I'd taken. I couldn't remember much, but at least I reached the bottom of the trail in one piece—which is more than I can say for Mr Show-off, Alan Gray. He tried to do lots of fancy moves and landed at the end of the trail on his

bottom with one leg in front of him, the other behind, and his poles lying about three metres away. He wasn't hurt, but he made three other boys crash into him, and a fourth fall over one of his poles.

I shook my head and got on the ski lift again. Then I began my descent to the end of the slope, only this time I picked up speed. I could see that Alan and his pals had cleared away from the scene of their accident. Good, I thought, and skied happily until I realized that someone was right behind me and staying there.

I was being followed on skis.

"Alan, stop!" I yelled into the wind and snow. I was afraid to turn round, though. I was sure I'd lose my balance.

By the time we reached the bottom of the trail, I was completely unnerved. "*Stop* it!" I yelled again. Only this time I did turn round, and of course I fell.

Someone fell on top of me.

I looked over my shoulder and right into the eyes of . . . a gorgeous guy.

It wasn't Alan at all.

"Oh, no!" I cried. "I'm so sorry!"

"Don't be," said the boy. "It wasn't your fault. It was mine. I don't have very good control over these skis yet. I knew I was right behind you but I couldn't help it."

"Well, that's okay." I was all out of breath.

And I couldn't tell if it was because of our accident, or because of the amazing face I was gazing at.

Somehow, the two of us managed to untangle ourselves and stand up. As soon as we did, we fell again. We burst out laughing.

"This is like a Laurel and Hardy film," said the boy.

I had to stop laughing so that I could catch my breath.

When we were on our feet and had calmed down, the boy said, "My name's Pierre. Pierre D'Amboise."

"I'm Stacey McGill," I told him.

Here's a fact: It's very difficult to shake hands when you're wearing ski mittens. They're so puffy and fat it's like shaking hands with giant marshmallows.

"Where are you from?" Pierre asked me as we panted our way to the ski lift.

"Stoneybrook, Connecticut," I answered. "My whole school is here. I'm in the eighth grade."

"I'm in the eighth, too," said Pierre. "My class is here for the week. We're from Dixville Falls. That's further north. Almost in Canada."

"Wow!" I said. "Canada. Are you French Canadian? I mean, is your family French Canadian?"

"No. We're French French. My parents grew up in Paris, but just after they got married, they

moved to the States. I've always lived in Vermont.
I hardly speak any French, and I learn Italian at
school. I'm a real embarrassment to my parents."

I laughed. "Do you speak *any* French?"

"Chevrolet coupé."

That time I laughed so hard I nearly fell over.
Ski boots tip you forward, and it's not easy to
laugh all tipped over on skis in slippery snow.

Pierre caught me by the arm and kept me
upright. "Come on," he said. "It's our turn."

We were at the head of the queue for the ski lift,
and we let ourselves be scooped up and carried to
the top of the slope. Then we skied down
together. Or sort of together, since neither of us is
very good. At least we didn't crash into each other
at the bottom.

Much as I wanted to make another run with
Pierre, I knew that it was time for me to check on
Miss Halliday and the kids. I explained to Pierre
what I had to do, and then I set off for the
snowbunny group. When I reached it, I found
fifteen exuberant children, most of whom were
sure they were just about ready to enter the next
Winter Olympics.

"How's everything going?" I asked Miss
Halliday.

"Oh, just fine," she replied. "The children are
great. So enthusiastic."

"No problems?"

"No. The instructor's great, too."

"Okay. Do you mind if I go back to the slopes? I want to um, practise some more."

"Go ahead. We're doing fine here."

"Thanks, Miss Halliday!" I called as I made my way back to the ski lift. All I could think about as I struggled along was Pierre.

Pierre D'Amboise. The name alone made me feel ultrasophisticated, almost continental. I pictured Pierre's sparkling eyes, his brown hair with the streaks of blond in it. (Had he been out in the sun recently? On some faraway island, perhaps?) Then I remembered his voice. It was changing, acquiring that deepness.

I thought over the other boys I've known—the boys at school, the boys I'd met at the Sea City beach. And I decided that Pierre was the nicest, the most fun, and—if things went my way— probably my first serious crush. Any past crushes suddenly didn't count.

9th
CHAPTER

Mallory
⚓

Wednesday morning

Hi, Mary Anne. I hope it's okay if I
take my notes for you right out of my journal,
because that's what I'm doing. Okay, here's
what happened today:

Wednesday started with an awful
announcement at breakfast. Our deputy-
head made it. He stood up and said
in this cheery voice, "SMS pupils, I am
pleased to announce that this year, on
Friday night, an all-school dance will be
held in the lodge's grand ballroom. The
dance will be hosted by the Georges for
all pupils here at the lodge. You'll have
a chance to meet some new people, but
mostly to end your week in Hooksett
Crossing with an evening of fun."

Fun? Was he kidding? Oh, horrors.
Friday was going to be the worst night
of my life....

This is the truth about dances: I hate them. Well, no, that's not quite true. It's more that I'm afraid of them. Actually, it's more that I'm afraid of dancing and of boys. You see, I don't know how to dance. And I hardly ever spend time with boys except my brothers and boys that I babysit for, and they don't count. Not in the Game of Boys.

When the deputy-head made that announcement I thought I was going to faint right in the middle of the dining hall. Before he had even finished speaking I had grown so pale that Jessi had leaned over, put her hand on my arm, and exclaimed in a loud whisper, "Mal! Are you okay?"

I swallowed a couple of times. "Yes. I'll be fine," I replied, but my voice came out sounding choked.

"Are you sure?" asked Jessi. "What's the matter?"

"Nothing," I whispered.

Oh, no. A dance. A *dance*! I couldn't think of worse news. Well, a blizzard might be worse. Getting snowed into a building with Alan "Show-off" Gray would definitely be worse. But an all-school dance was at the top of the list of things I didn't want.

Straight away I began to think of ways to get out of going. Maybe the dance wasn't compulsory. If it wasn't, I could hide somewhere and write in my diary or read. If it was, well . . . maybe I could pretend to be ill. Come to think of it, I probably wouldn't have to do much pretending. Just thinking about the dance made me feel ill.

I looked around our breakfast table. There were the sixteen children. Pinky's bandage had been removed, and her foot was better, although not as strong as the doctor had hoped, so he had said she could walk on her foot, but couldn't go skiing or skating until the next day. And Miss Weber and Mr Dougherty were back. And Miss Weber's arm was in a plaster cast and sling, and Mr Dougherty's ribs were strapped up. You couldn't see that, of course. The only sign of his injuries was the slow, painful way in which he walked. Neither teacher was in tip-top shape.

Scattered among the children were Miss Halliday and my friends. I noticed that Mary Anne was sitting as far from Miss Halliday as she could. Opposite me was Jessi. We needed to talk about our snow sculpture, since the contest was that afternoon. Before we'd left Stoneybrook, Jessi had been really excited about the project. (We'd planned to sculpt a pair of ballet slippers with feet in them.) Now, every time I mentioned the contest, Jessi began to talk about things like frostbite and her toes and her dancing career. Further down the table, Claudia and Stacey were having a deep discussion about something, and Dawn was trying to get Pinky to finish her breakfast.

Kristy, sitting near the middle of the table next to Miss Halliday, stood up and tapped her knife on her glass of orange juice.

"Attention!" she called. "Can I have your attention?"

The dining hall quietened down—but not enough, so Kristy handed the knife to Miss Halliday, who tapped for her, while Kristy stood up on her chair.

"ATTENTION!" she called.

Since it was the second announcement of the meal, no one was very keen to stop talking.

But when Kristy finally yelled, "*ATTENTION, PLEASE!*" the room grew silent. "Thank you," said Kristy. "I want to announce that the ice-skating contest will be held this morning. It will begin at ten-thirty. If you want to participate, please be at the pond about fifteen minutes early. The snow-sculpture contest will be held in the afternoon. Please arrive by two-fifteen so we can start at two-thirty. The contest will take place on the lawn in front of the lodge. One last thing. The skiing events will be held on Friday. Remember that you can have free lessons with the instructors here. If you don't want lessons, then practise, practise, practise, okay?"

"Okay!" replied a few kids.

Kristy sat down, looking flushed. She certainly was taking her job seriously.

"Well," Jessi said to me, "what are you going to do this morning?"

"I'm not sure. What are you going to do?"

"Work on the talent sh—Oh, that reminds me. I've got to make an announcement, too."

As you can probably guess, it took even longer for Jessi to get everyone's attention than it had taken Kristy. In fact, Miss Halliday had to blow her gym whistle to make us be quiet. At last Jessi, who stood on her chair like Kristy in order to be heard, said, "Sorry to interrupt you again, but I want to announce that auditions for the talent show will be held in the grand ballroom this afternoon as soon as the snow-sculpture contest is over. If you want to be in the show but don't know what to do, come to the auditions anyway, because I've got some ideas. Thank you."

Jessi sat down. The deputy head stood up. "I would like to announce," he said, "that there will be no further announcements."

Everyone cheered. And then people began to leave the dining hall. I was on my own for the morning. Jessi had her work to do. Kristy, Claudia, and Dawn were going to be in the ice-skating contest, Mary Anne was busy moping and working on *her* project, and Stacey seemed to be in an awful rush to get somewhere. Where? I wondered.

Then I remembered my *own* project. I tore up to our dormitory, slipped my diary out of its hiding place under my mattress, and took it down to the common room to write about the morning's events.

This was my diary project: I planned to work hard on my writing, since I want to become an author one day. A big place with a lot of new people and activities was perfect for sharpening my observational skills. I planned to play Harriet from *Harriet the Spy*, just like I'd done when my friends and I went on a cruise to the Bahamas and then travelled to Disney World. Only I intended to be a better spy than Harriet. For one thing, I wasn't going to get caught. For another, I was going to be such a keen observer that my diary would be filled only with the truth. I would never, ever read something into a situation that wasn't really there.

For a while, I just sat in the common room and wrote about my feelings and reactions to what had gone on so far that morning. I started off with:

The children are in very good moods today, except for Pinky, who is **angry because** she can't go skiing or skating until tomorrow. I'm really surprised at how quickly the kids bounced back from the accident. My mum once said that children are resilient. She should know, since she's got eight of them.

85

Mallory

Then I began observing what was going on in the common room:

Mary Anne is **really missing** Logan. I'm pretty sure about this because I peeked at what she was writing, and instead of filling her pages with information about Hooksett Crossing and Leicester Lodge, she's writing things like:

Mary Anne and Logan   Mary Anne Bruno
Mrs. L. Bruno   Logan Spier (hmm...)
Mary Anne Spier-Bruno XXX, OOO
♡♡♡ Logan, my love, my one and only ♡♡♡

Every now and then she gets hold of herself and writes about her project, but not very often. From what I can see of her notes, this lodge is haunted! I never knew that before. But maybe that explains the white thing I saw in the corner of our dorm last night. Then again, it might just have been Stacey's bathrobe, hanging on a hook.

When I got bored with the common room, I decided to try some serious spying. I carried my notebook into the dining hall. It was empty (of course), and so big that my footsteps echoed, so I had to tiptoe. Cautiously, I approached the kitchen. Swinging double doors lead into it and one door was propped open. I peeped around it and saw several of the cook's helpers preparing lunch. Then I saw the cook himself. He's an old man with not much hair, a stubbly beard, and one top tooth missing. Up until now I'd thought he'd seemed really nice. But when I peeped in at him, this is what was going on:

The cook is sprinkling something into a vat of soup. The stuff is coming from a jar that's not labelled. I think it is poison. And now he's picking up a huge knife. Oh, no. The cook is crazy. He may be trying to kill us all!

I fled back to the common room, where Pinky, Joey, Ginnie, and Bryce were playing a silly board game called Operation. Ginnie and Joey were yelling at Pinky and she was having a temper tantrum. I have a feeling Pinky isn't too popular.

By this time I had to go to the toilet. I used the ladies' downstairs, and who should I see in there, but Miss Halliday. And she was crying:

Mallory

I know Miss Halliday is crying, even though she's trying to cover it up. She keeps dabbing at her eyes with a wet paper towel and saying, "Isn't this silly? I've worn contacts for years and they still give me trouble."

But I know better. Miss Halliday's contacts aren't bothering her. She's suffering from unrequited love. She has a crush on the deputy-head, but he isn't interested in her. Guess who else has a crush on someone?

Stacey. She likes a boy! I saw them kissing!!

Gosh. My diary was really thrilling! I would have to find a better hiding place for it than under my mattress. At home, too. If my little brothers or sisters ever found this, they would read things that are *far* too mature for them.

10th CHAPTER

Dawn

Wednesday morning

Here are my notes, Mary Anne. I'm being as honest as possible, but I hope you don't put everything I write into your book for Logan. Some of this stuff is embarrassing. He doesn't really need to know all of it, so use your good judgement and take out the worst stuff, okay?

This was not a good day for me, as you well know, since you were part of the problem. (No offence. Just being honest. That's what

Dawn

you asked for.) Anyway, the ice-skating competition was a disaster. I am so humiliated....

When we woke up on Wednesday it was still snowing—not hard, just enough to make Kristy really worried.

"How can we hold the sculpture contest this afternoon?" she cried. "The snow will just keep covering up everyone's work. It'll be a disaster."

"Why don't you wait until this afternoon to decide whether to call off the contest?" Miss Halliday suggested at breakfast. "It's hardly snowing at all, Kristy. I think you should announce the contest anyway. If you have to call it off—and I doubt you will—you can announce the change in schedule at lunchtime. At the moment the snow seems to be letting up."

So Kristy made her announcements. As soon as breakfast was over, she and Claud and I got our skates and headed for the pond so that we could practise before the contest began. We found quite a few other kids there, too. I'm no skater, but I'm not bad. I practised skating fast, skating backwards, and doing figure-of-eights. That's about the best I can do.

There were to be three parts to the contest. The first part was speed. Each person in each team would be timed to see how fast he or she could skate fifty metres. It was the skating version of the fifty-metre sprint. The team with the fastest skater would earn one point. Next was a sort of relay race. The teams would divide into two, half of each team standing on one side of the pond, the other halves opposite them. Then we were given ten minutes in which to see how many times the members of each team could carry a baton back and forth across the ice. If everyone in a team had crossed before the time was up, they just started again. That's why it didn't matter whether the Red and the Blue Teams were evenly represented.

Again, the team that made the most trips across the pond earned a point. The tiebreaker event (if it was needed) was a sort of obstacle course. Ten members from each team were chosen to do the following: skate backwards to the middle of the pond, execute a figure-of-eight, then continue to the opposite side, skating in and out of a row of coffee tins. The team that finished first won a point, and the team that earned two out of three points was the overall winner of the competition.

Kristy got things rolling promptly at ten-thirty.

"All right, teams," she said, facing the kids who had gathered. (Thirty-one Red Team members and twenty-eight Blue Team members were there.) "Our first event is speed skating. All of you may take part."

Kristy went on to explain the rules. Then she organized us into two long lines, handed a stopwatch to Mr Cheney, the scorekeeper, and took her place at the head of the line of Blue Team members. Rick Chow stood at the head of the Red Team line. Mr Cheney tossed a coin, and our team, the Blue Team, won the right to go first.

So Kristy sailed across the ice to the flag that had been placed fifty metres out on the pond. For someone short, she is really fast. She made excellent time. Then Rick Chow took his turn. He wasn't as fast as Kristy.

You might think that watching fifty-nine kids skate out to a flag one at a time would get boring after a while, but it didn't. We just kept cheering and cheering. And each time someone beat the best score, Mr Cheney would call out the new time. It was pretty exciting.

I waited nervously for my turn, my heart pumping, and the adrenaline flowing through my body. I concentrated so hard on that flag across the ice that Mr Cheney had to say, "On your marks, get set, go!" three times before I heard him. Then I went whizzing off—and halfway to the flag I hit a bump on the ice, tripped, and fell. I knew I had to get up and keep going, so I did. I also knew I had just contributed the slowest time so far to our team.

I was right.

But our team won anyway. A girl called Andrea Kirkland was the fastest.

As we were getting ready for the relay race, Kristy thumped me on the back, said not to worry, and wished me better luck in the next event. I felt relieved—until I saw two seventh-graders from the other team pointing at me and laughing.

I ignored them. Mum says I'm like a duck in a storm. Insults roll right off my back like raindrops off a duck's feathers. I geared myself up for the relay race, giving myself a silent pep talk.

The race began. The cheering was loud and constant since the skaters in both teams kept going and going at the same time. When Paul

Friedman finally slapped the baton into my hand—I dropped it! My mittens were so fat and clumsy. But I picked it right up and skated out across the ice. This time I don't know how I fell, but I did. One second I was skating along, the next second I was on my hands and knees. It took me a while to get up and find the baton. I lost a lot of time for my team.

And the Red Team won. Now we would have to hold the tiebreaker event.

"Teams!" Kristy cried, standing in front of the participants. "Get ready for the tiebreaker. I want each team captain—that's you and me, Rick—"

("Never," said Rick under his breath.)

"—to pick ten people to take part in this, the final event."

We divided into teams and Kristy looked over the kids on our team. Then she carefully picked ten people.

I wasn't one of them.

I watched the tiebreaker silently, unable to cheer. I just didn't have any cheers in me. When our team finally lost the ice-skating competition, two kids actually came up to me and said sarcastically, "Good work, Dawn!"

My cheeks began to burn. Why were they insulting me? Anyone could fall . . . twice . . . and drop the baton.

I was about to go back to the dormitory for a

94

while when Kristy announced practice for the snowball fight. Considering what had happened when I tried to ice-skate, I decided I'd better not miss a practice. So I went.

The mock fight took place at the edge of some woods not far from the skating pond. The first thing that happened when it began was that Alan Gray hit me in the face with a snowball and then stuffed another one down the back of my ski jacket.

"Ha, ha!" he sang. "Ha, ha. Ha, ha-ha, ha, ha!"

I can't stand it when people do that. Worse still, a crowd of other kids had seen what Alan had done. They were laughing, too. I was surrounded by ha-has. I needed to escape. So I simply left the fight. Since there was still some time before lunch, I decided to get a pair of boots and skis and take a couple of runs down the mountain to clear my head and drive away some of the anger I could feel building up.

I'm a pretty good skier (yes, you can ski in California, and Dad took us to Vail in Colorado, a couple of times), so I headed for the intermediate trails, expecting to go on the advanced ones later that afternoon.

But I didn't get any further than the ski lift. I fell trying to get *on* it. (Most people, if they're going to fall, fall getting off.) The kids in the queue behind me sniggered.

95

Okay. Enough was enough. Usually I don't care what anyone says or thinks about me, but one too many people had laughed at me that morning. In a huff, I returned the boots, skis, and poles, and marched back to the lodge. I stamped into the common room and right over to Mary Anne, who was writing in that book for Logan.

"Well, congratulate me!" I said.

Mary Anne looked up, blinking her eyes. "Huh?"

"Congratulate me."

"For what?"

"For walking from the ski hire office to the lodge without falling down."

Mary Anne paused. At last she said, "I'm not—Did you have a bad morning or something?"

"Yes, I had a bad morning." I flopped into an armchair next to Mary Anne.

"What happened?"

I gave Mary Anne the grisly details—from falling on the ice to falling off the ski lift. I waited expectantly for the sympathy to come pouring out, since Mary Anne is the most sensitive, caring person I know, and also, with a little luck, my future stepsister.

But the words that came out of Mary Anne's mouth were, "Do you have any idea how far Aruba is from Hooksett Crossing?"

My jaw must have dropped because Mary Anne immediately said "What? What's wrong?"

"*What's wrong?*" I exploded. "I'm sitting here pouring my heart out to you—which, by the way, I don't do very often—and all you can think of is your precious Logan. Have you thought of anything or anyone else since we left Stoneybrook?"

Mary Anne narrowed her eyes at me. She doesn't lose her temper often, but she's human, after all. She just has a longer-than-usual, very slow-burning fuse. I had a feeling I'd reached the end of it.

I was right.

POW!

Mary Anne let loose. "Of *course* I've thought of other things," she cried. "I've been working on my project . . . sort of . . . and rescuing children, and—"

"Oh, forget it," I snapped. "You still didn't hear a word I said. And friends are supposed to listen when they're needed."

"Then I suppose I'm not much of a friend, am I?"

"I suppose not."

"Fine."

"You're fired as my bunk-mate."

"You can't fire me, because I fire you."

Well, it didn't matter who fired whom. All I know is that I stamped up to our dormitory, yanked the blankets and sheets off my bed, and made up the empty bed on the bunk beneath Pinky's.

Dawn

I decided that I was not speaking to Miss Mary
Anne Spier, my ex-bunk-mate and former friend.

11th CHAPTER

Mary Anne

Wednesday afternoon

Ooh, I am so angry with Dawn Schafer. Logan, you should have heard her this morning. I don't know what got into her. She had a bad day and she took it out on me. Not only is that unlike Dawn, but it wasn't fair. If she wants someone to listen to her so much, she should get a dog. Or a parrot, so it could talk back to her. Well, maybe that's not fair, either. Maybe I should have listened to her. I'm her best friend, after all. On the other hand, I was having problems of my own. Not serious ones. I mean, not too serious. Oh, I don't know....

99

Wednesday wasn't exactly the best day of my week at the lodge, although it started off okay. After breakfast I decided to interview three of the oldest employees at the lodge. One was Marie Castleman, the head housekeeper, who was at least seventy-five years old; one was Teensy Mooseman, whose real name is Rebeccah, but no one calls her that, and who was in charge of all the gardeners and handymen, and who was also about seventy-five; and the last one was Curtis Oates, the head cook, who looked a little younger than Marie and Teensy—maybe seventy or so.

I started with Marie, mainly because as I was leaving the library, I passed her office and saw her in there.

"Excuse me," I said, knocking lightly on the doorframe.

Marie looked up. "Yes?" Her grey hair was frizzy, she wore gold-rimmed granny glasses, and she was as skinny as a weasel. But what I couldn't help noticing first were her ears. They were pierced, and must have been pierced for decades, and Marie must have worn very heavy earrings in them for all those decades because now her earlobes were, well, let's just say droopy.

"Um, hello, I'm Mary Anne Spier," I said. "I'm writing a report about Hooksett Crossing and Leicester Lodge, and Mrs George said you've worked here for a long time and—"

"Only since nineteen-thirty," Marie interrupted proudly.

"Since nineteen-thirty. Wow!"

Marie smiled. She put her pen down and beckoned to me to come in and sit down. I did, and she began talking straight away, so I began taking notes. "The lodge was only ten years old when I began working here," she said. "The Georges didn't own it then, of course. They weren't even born then. And the lodge was nowhere near this size. Huge additions were built in the forties and fifties."

I let Marie talk for almost fifteen minutes before I said, "I heard the lodge has a ghost."

Silence.

"I—I read that in Mr George's book," I ventured.

Marie sniffed. "I don't take any notice of such things."

"But have you ever seen a ghost here? Or anything weird?"

"Never. Not once," Marie replied quickly.

I nodded. "Well, thank you very much. I really appreciate your talking to me. It was a big help."

"Any time." Marie smiled again. Was it a smile of relief? I wondered. A smile because I hadn't pressed the ghost issue?

I found Curtis Oates in the kitchen, showing a new cook how to make tuna salad for eight hundred. When I saw that he was busy, I started

101

to back out of the double doors, but Curtis looked up and smiled. He's got a tooth missing, which is something I just can't stand. I mean, in adults. I'm a firm believer in dentures.

"Well," I said, "I wanted to interview you for my essay on Hooksett Crossing and the lodge, but you're busy, so I'll come back later."

"Oh, now hang on," Curtis replied. "I'm at a good place to stop. I was just getting ready to take a coffee break. Do you drink coffee?"

"Uh, no. Thanks." I tried to picture the look on my father's face if he were to catch me drinking coffee. He's often said that coffee will prevent me from growing—and I'm not that tall to begin with.

Curtis poured himself a cup of coffee and we sat opposite each other at a butcher's block table where someone had been chopping onions. The onions made my eyes run, but they didn't seem to effect Curtis.

I asked Curtis what Hooksett Crossing had been like when he was a boy, and he told me all about it and also how the town had changed during the Depression, and again during World War II. Then he told me how the Georges had bought the lodge in 1963. Finally I asked my big question—what about the ghost?

Curtis suddenly lost the power of speech. He became as unresponsive as when I'd asked him about the ghost the last time. So I thanked him

102

(with onion tears welling up in my eyes), and went off in search of Teensy Mooseman.

Teensy is not very hard to find in winter, since there isn't a lot of gardening and outside work to be done. I headed for the boiler room, because, according to Mrs George, the boiler breaks down with great regularity all winter long. Sure enough, there was Teensy and two repair people. Despite her age, Teensy was wearing blue denim overalls, a checked shirt, and a paint-spattered baseball cap.

Teensy was just as eager to talk as Marie and Curtis had been—until I asked the ghost question. Then she shut up. All I could get out of her was, "No such things as ghosts." (Actually, she said, "No setch things as ghosts.") This was getting me nowhere. And the more people avoided the ghost subject, the more I wanted to hear about it.

I decided I should talk to Mr George, since he'd devoted three chapters in his book to the ghost. And Mr George did turn out to be helpful. At least he would talk.

"The ghost story," he said, "seems to have stemmed from the death of a visitor to the lodge in the late nineteen-thirties. One morning he was found dead in his bath. No one knew what had happened to him. But when his relatives heard the news, they seemed awfully relieved. They seemed to think he was evil. One went so far as to say he was in league with the devil. And none of

103

them would agree to take his body away for burial, so he was buried in the woods here. The owner of the lodge took pity on the dead man. But as soon as he'd been laid to rest, visitors and workers here began reporting odd occurrences."

"Like what?" I asked.

"Oh, the usual. Nothing they couldn't have read in a mystery book—windows that opened themselves on rainy nights, vague white figures drifting down dark hallways or staircases" (I shivered), "odd moaning noises, also usually at night. That sort of thing."

"And what do you think?" I asked.

"I think," Mr George answered with a smile, "that my wife and I have owned the lodge for over twenty years and haven't experienced *any* of those things. Not one. A few of our guests have. And Curtis had quite a scare one night, but we think people's imaginations tend to run away with them. That's all."

I asked what kind of scare Curtis had had, and Mr George said something about his mistaking a pile of laundry for a ghost. Not too interesting. So I went back to the common room and started to write up the notes from my interviews. I couldn't concentrate, though. No matter how hard I tried to work, I kept finding myself picturing Logan and that gorgeous girl doing all sorts of island things together—snorkelling, waterskiing, tanning . . . kissing.

A horrible feeling settled in the pit of my stomach. And just when the feeling was at its worst, Dawn came back to the lodge, slumped into a chair, and picked a fight with me. Honestly. She really did. She accused me of being insensitive, and then she fired me as her bunk-mate and moved all her things to the empty bed under Pinky's.

What a baby. Why did I ever think she was one of my best friends?

When Dawn went off on a huff, I moved to one of the two chairs hidden in a corner of the common room. They were facing a window, which meant their backs were to the rest of the room. Perfect. I didn't feel like looking at anyone or talking to anybody.

Mary Anne

Once again, I tried to work. I had written exactly three sentences when someone sat down in the chair next to me. For a long time, I managed not to look at the person. I wanted to be alone, and I hoped that whoever it was would go away.

But the person didn't leave. However, he (or she) didn't speak to me, either. And after a while I became so curious about this quiet person who was probably as depressed as I was that I just had to look over and see who it was.

When I did, I saw . . . Miss Halliday.

Yikes!

I started to leave, realizing that Miss Halliday didn't even know I was there. Or if she did, she didn't care. She looked as thoughtful and as sad as I probably looked.

As quietly as I could, I gathered up my things. I was just starting to tiptoe away, when Miss Halliday *spoke to me*.

"You don't have to leave," she said.

"Oh, that's okay. I was just . . . just . . ." What *was* I doing? Escaping?

"You look rather sad," Miss Halliday observed.

"So do you," I couldn't help replying.

"I miss someone," Miss Halliday said simply.

"Me, too," I whispered.

"Really? Who?"

This didn't sound like the screaming gym teacher I remembered, so I told her about Logan. Then *she* told me about her fiancé. He was a

106

reporter for our Stoneybrook newspaper, and she was really missing him. It turned out that they'd never been separated for more than a couple of days.

I must have had a funny look on my face because after a pause, Miss Halliday said, "You know, Mary Anne, I have a feeling that you think I don't like you."

I was completely taken aback, but this quiet Miss Halliday seemed pretty easy to talk to, so I found the courage to say, "That's . . . that's true. I'm so bad at sports. I know I was a really frustrating gym student. I suppose I do think you don't like me. Actually, I think you hate me."

"Oh, Mary Anne, no. I'm sorry. I pushed you last year, that's true, because I wanted you to try your hardest. But I know that not everyone is a born athlete. In fact, I admired you because you kept trying. Even when I asked you to do difficult things."

Really? Wow! I felt much better—about everything, even my fight with Dawn. I knew we'd make up sooner or later. And when Jessi asked me if I'd help the children rehearse a turn for the talent show, I said yes straight away.

The day was looking brighter.

12th CHAPTER

Kristy

Wednesday

Sorry, Mary Anne, but I don't have time to write much for you. I'm too busy with the Winter War. This morning we held the ice-skating competition, then I started a practice snowball fight, and while that was going on, I organized a snowman-building contest for the Conway Cove kids. They needed something special to do. This afternoon is the snow-sculpture competition, then more ski practice.

Gotta go. 'Bye!

Whew! Tuesday was easy compared to Wednesday. With the Winter War underway I was running around like a headless chicken. (I know that's a disgusting analogy but my stepfather says it all the time.)

The first event of the day was the skating contest, which my team *lost*. I had fully expected to win. There were some really good athletes on my team, but old Dawn was completely hopeless. I didn't know she was so clumsy. If I *had* known, I wouldn't have encouraged her to enter the contests. And I was certainly going to stop asking Mary Anne to take part. We didn't need another failure. I know that sounds mean but, well, I wanted to *win*. I was the team captain and I like winning, okay? What's wrong with that?

As I said in my notes for Mary Anne's book, after we lost the ice-skating event, I started a snowball fight so the kids could practise for the real thing the next day. Once that was underway, I rounded up the Conway Cove children and asked them if they wanted to have a snowman-building competition. Nine of them did, so I directed them to the area on the front lawn near where the snow sculptures would be built in the afternoon.

I should mention here that it had *finally* stopped snowing. I should also mention that the sky was darker than it had been when we'd woken up in the morning, and guess what the weather report forecast: a riproaring storm (I got the weather report from Teensy Mooseman) that was supposed to begin late on Thursday night.

Anyway, here are the children who wanted to build snowmen: Renée, Corey, Kara, Valerie, Frankie, Ian, Amber, Ryan, and Kathie. Bryce, Joey, Ginnie, and Pinky were playing inside, and the others were off skiing.

I needed someone to help me with this last-minute contest, and it wasn't easy finding a BSC member who was free. Jessi, Mal, and Mary Anne were working on their projects, Dawn had gone off angry, and Stacey was nowhere to be found. Finally I had to drag Claud away from the snowball fight.

"Come on," I said. "It'll be good practice for judging the snow sculptures this afternoon. I *really* need you. Everyone else is busy, angry with me, or has disappeared."

Reluctantly, Claudia came with me.

"All right," I said to the children, "each of you has until fifteen minutes before lunchtime to build a snowman. You can use any props you want—scarves or hats or sticks or whatever. Claudia will choose the winning snowman."

"Snow *person*," spoke up Kara. "It doesn't have to be a man, you know."

And Frankie asked, "What does the winner get?"

Hmm. Good question. The winners of the

110

Winter War were each going to get a coupon for a free slice of pizza at the Pizza Pan back in Stoneybrook. But what could we give the Conway Cove winner?

"I know!" Claudia cried suddenly. "But I can't tell you what it is. It'll be a surprise."

"What if we don't like it?" asked Amber.

Yes, I thought.

But all Claud would say was, "Trust me. It's good."

So, looking doubtful, the children got to work on their snowmen. They rolled and patted the snow. Sometimes they needed help. Corey seemed to think that bigger was better and rolled three balls that were so huge and heavy he needed both Claudia and me to help him put the middle part on the bottom, and the head on the middle part.

Kara worked diligently on a snow woman who was wearing a long skirt.

And Ian made a snow Martian.

Once the bodies were built, the children began running into the hotel for props. And Claud and I began laughing. Those children were making really imaginative snow creatures. Valerie put glasses on hers. Renée dressed hers in Mr Dougherty's ski jacket. Kara stuck boots under the skirt of the snow woman. Ian made tinfoil antennae for his Martian.

Fifteen minutes before lunchtime I shouted, "Time's up, everyone!"

111

"Oh," groaned at least half the children.

"We're not finished," complained Ryan.

"Sorry," I replied. "Our judge needs a few minutes to make her decision. Everyone stand next to your snowma—snow creature."

Obediently, the children stopped their work.

Claudia paced up and down in front of the nine masterpieces, her hands behind her back, her brow furrowed. She was deep in thought. Was this how she planned to look when she judged our snow sculptures?

At long last (when there were only about ten minutes left before lunch), Claudia stopped her pacing, stood beside me, and said, "I am pleased to announce that third in place is Frankie and his

snow farmer. In second place is Ian and his snow Martian. And finally . . . the grand-prize winner is Kara and her snow woman!"

"Hurray!" cried Kara.

The other children tried to smile, but they weren't very successful. "Now don't anyone go away," said Claud. "Wait right here for the prizes. All of you."

"What? What prizes?" asked the children as Claud dashed inside.

"I have no idea," I replied honestly.

When Claudia returned, she was carrying a Polaroid camera. She took a photo of each child with his or her creation. By the end of the day, the photos were displayed in the common room with a yellow ribbon under Frankie's picture, a red one under Ian's, and a huge blue one under Kara's. You should have seen the looks on the children's faces when they saw the display. For the rest of the week, they kept hanging around it, especially Kara. I had to hand it to Claud. For someone who thinks she isn't clever, she comes up with really good ideas.

By two-fifteen, when the snow-sculpture contest was getting underway, the sky was so heavy with clouds that I wouldn't have been surprised if it had fallen down, just like Chicken Licken was afraid of. Of course it didn't. And the snow held off, too.

Fifteen minutes later, I found myself saying, "The snow-sculpture contest will now begin! You have an hour to work on your sculptures. The creators of the best sculpture will win this event for their team. And for those of you who don't know, the Red Team won the skating contest this morning. Okay, teams, get to work!"

All across the lawn, groups of kids began shaping mounds of snow. Very few contestants were working alone. In fact, Ashley Wyeth and a sixth-grade boy I didn't know were the only ones.

I thought the Conway Cove children had been serious snow-person builders this morning, but I wasn't prepared for us older kids. Lots of us were equipped with buckets of water to help freeze the snow into shapes. We had no rules apart from the time limit.

I was working with Dawn and Stacey on a giant teddy bear. (Dawn was barely speaking to me.) Not far away Jessi and Mal were working on something that I couldn't identify. Good. They were in the other team. I hoped Claud wouldn't be able to identify it, either.

The hour flew by so quickly that when Claudia told me the time was up, I could hardly believe it. Then Claud began her pacing again. She and Mr Cheney, the co-judge, examined each sculpture thoroughly. I grew extremely impatient waiting for their decision.

After what seemed like hours, Claudia said, "It

wasn't easy, but we've decided that the winning sculpture is Troy Parker and Amelia White's Cheshire Cat from *Alice in Wonderland.*

Bother! I should have known better than to agree to let Claud judge the contest. Of course she'd chosen a sculpture by Red Team members. My team had lost *again.* The only way we could win the Winter War now was if we beat the Red Team in every other contest.

Blow!

I couldn't help giving Claud a dirty look.

And I noticed that I wasn't the only one doing so. Ashley looked pretty disgusted herself. And no wonder. She *is* one of the best artists in the school, not to mention a member of the Blue Team and one of Claud's good friends. I know she had expected Claud to choose hers as the winning entry in the contest.

I sighed deeply. My team just *had* to win the war. Suddenly energized, I announced, "Don't forget ski practice, everybody. Take a lesson or just go up on the slopes. You've only got until Friday to get yourselves in top form."

Then I joined Claud. "Going skiing now?" I asked her.

"I don't know. Maybe. I'm a bit tired."

"I suppose you think you're so good you don't need to practise."

"That's not true!" exclaimed Claud. "I may be good, but I'm not stuck up."

"Are you calling me stuck-up?"

"*NO*."

"Well, I'm going to take some runs. Maybe even a lesson."

"Okay."

"Okay."

"*Okay*."

For the rest of the afternoon, Claudia and I skied the advanced trails under the watchful eyes of instructors. I hated to admit that Claud was better than me—but she was. Everyone knew that she was the best skier in our whole school, and I was second best.

Even so, I couldn't help yelling out to her as we swooshed down a slope, "Our team's going to annihilate your team on Friday, Kishi!"

13th CHAPTER

Claudia

Wensday afternon

I will never juge anything agian
-- unless I'm juging totle strangers.
The snow sclupture contest was
awfal all afternoon kristy tryed to be
really nice to me I know she
whanted me to choose her teddy bear
as the winning sclupture but it was
just too twee for words. As juge I
no better than to look for somthing
twee. I was looking for a well planned,
well done peice of work. The cheshur
cat fit the bill. It was realistic
and just a little bite mean looking.
Ahsley is made at me too.

I'd just love to see what Kristy wrote about the contest. I bet it's pretty different from what I wrote. I know she thinks I chose the Cheshire Cat because it won another contest for the Red Team, but that's just not true. I honestly thought it was the best sculpture, and Mr Cheney, the co-judge, agreed with me.

I decided to ignore Kristy and Ashley and their angry, flashing eyes and take a free skiing lesson. Kristy practically dared me to, anyway. I could have practised on my own, but I thought, here I am at a ski resort with good instructors. I should take advantage of them. Maybe I can refine my technique.

So I went to the ski hire office and asked about

lessons for advanced skiers. The woman there told me that a class was starting in just ten minutes.

"Great!" I exclaimed. "Thanks!"

I took the ski lift to the top of the expert slope and there I found three kids from my team plus a few other people—and the most amazing-looking instructor in the history of skiing. His face was ruddy from being outdoors all day. His hair was blond and curly, his eyes were pale blue, and—best of all—he spoke with an accent.

"Hello," he greeted us. All of us were awestruck, especially the girls. "My name eez Guy." (He pronounced his name so that it rhymed with "ski".) "I am your eenstroctor. I trost zat you are very goode skiers."

"Oh, *very*," I couldn't help replying.

Guy smiled, showing a row of perfectly straight sparkly white teeth. "Excellent. Zen let us get on wiss sings."

Sings? Oh, *things*.

"First, I woode like to see each of you take a ron down zee trail."

Where was Guy from? France? Switzerland? I couldn't think about anything except his gorgeous face and his intriguing accent. If only he were a little younger. He looked about twenty-five. Well, maybe that didn't matter. I could fall in love with an older man . . . couldn't I? It happens all the time. I mean, to other people.

119

The members of my skiing class were lining up to go down the expert trail. Guy spoke quietly to the first pupil and then she took off down the mountain. He watched her carefully. Then the next pupil went down, and then it was my turn.

"Zose are nice boots. Nice skis, too," said Guy approvingly, looking my equipment over. "Zose are not from zee lodge, are zey?"

"Oh, no," I replied. "They're mine. I go skiing all the time." (That wasn't *quite* true.) "I'm more comfortable with my own skis and stuff."

Guy nodded and smiled. "I onderstand. Now. Let me see whot you can do."

I drew in a deep breath and let it out slowly. I wanted to do my best for Guy.

So down I went. I concentrated very hard. I tried to remember everything I'd been taught. When I reached the bottom, I knew I'd performed well. I returned to Guy, feeling pretty pleased. But when I saw the expression on his face, my pleasure turned to joy.

"Marvellous!" he exclaimed. "Claudia, zat wozz wonderful!"

Claudia. He called me Claudia! I was pretty sure he'd been calling everyone else Miss or Mrs or Mr.

"Thanks—thanks, Guy," I said breathlessly.

Guy smiled. And then . . . he put his *hand* on my *arm.* "Let me jost geeve you a few hints. You can improve your speed by . . ."

120

I was listening to Guy. I really was. But I couldn't help noticing that not far from our group, another class was starting up. A young woman stood before a group of intent pupils. And one of those pupils was Kristy. She saw me at the same time I saw her.

Can you believe it? She actually stuck her tongue out at me. Right there in front of Guy and her instructor and all the pupils! Just because the Blue Team had lost in ice-skating and snow sculpture. Of course, it did mean that if the Blue Team were going to win the Winter War, they had to win the remaining three events. And that was pretty unlikely. (By the way, in case you're wondering, if the Red Team won the next event—which meant we'd won the war—the skiing competitions would be held on Friday anyway. They were too much fun to miss.)

"Claudia?" Guy was saying. He touched my arm again.

"Oh. Yes?" How could I concentrate if he was going to keep touching my arm?

"You need to change your pozeetion slightly. Like zees." Now Guy practically had his arms around me. I looked over at Kristy to see if she was watching us.

She was.

I wished I could have stuck my tongue out at her, but I am much too mature to do a thing like that when a handsome older man has his arms around me.

"Okay," I said to Guy. "I see what I'm supposed to do now."

"Goode. Now take anozzer ron down zee trail."

Anoz—? Oh, another run down the trail.

"All right," I said.

I let myself fly. There's nothing in the world so wonderful as that feeling of motion and speed as you sail along over snow. Unfortunately, I noticed that at the same time I set off, so did Kristy. She wasn't far away. And she began to edge towards me so that soon we were skiing side by side down the mountain. I really hate having someone so close to me when I'm on skis.

I thought that over and changed my mind when I realized that Guy could have been skiing two inches from me and I would have been delighted. But Kristy was several feet away and that was too close.

"Move over!" I shouted at her. The wind was in my face but she heard me anyway.

"Making you nervous?" she yelled back.

"No! You're in my way!"

"I'm not. And anyway, our team is going to annihilate your team on Friday, Kishi."

"No, you're not. Besides, it won't matter if you do because we're going to win the snowball fight tomorrow and then the war will be over."

Kristy shouted some sort of reply, but I put on a burst of speed and shot ahead, so I couldn't hear what she said. And I managed to stay ahead of her and even beat her back up the mountain again. Back to Guy . . . .

"Claudia! Again zat wozz magneefeecent. You are a chompion!"

A chompion? *Me?*

Guy took my hands in his (well, my fat mittens in his fat mittens) and said solemnly, "Next time, I want complete concentration. Onderstand? Do not let yourself be deestracted on zee trail. You weel be surprised at how moch better you can do."

"Okay," I said. At least, I think I said it I was looking into Guy's eyes, which were sparkly and bright. Then I looked at his lips and couldn't help imagining myself kissing them. I'm not sure whether any sound came from my own lips.

Something must have, though, because Guy said, "Very goode. Now go—and concentrate." He patted my shoulder.

Well, of course I went soaring down that mountain. Kristy dried to distract me again by skiing practically on my heels, but all I could think of was pleasing Guy. I was able to ignore Kristy completely and beat her back up the mountain again, where Guy put his arms across my shoulders and called me his star pupil.

I grinned from ear to ear. And then, unfortunately, I realized that after one more run down the mountain I would have to go back to the lodge. It was almost dinnertime, and I should probably help with the Conway Cove children.

So I said a sad goodbye to Guy and got ready for one last run.

"I weel see you tomorrow, no?" said Guy. "Anozzer lesson for my star pupeel?"

No? *Yes!* Yes, of course he would see me. I would do anything Guy wanted. I would go over a ski jump and turn a somersault in the air if he thought I could do it.

I tried to appear suave and sophisticated, though, so all I said was, "Of course. Tomorrow." I wished I could speak whatever Guy's native language was.

I was about halfway down the mountain when a thought struck me, a guilty thought. *Will Yamakawa.* He was a boy I'd met at Camp Mohawk and we had *really* hit it off. He didn't go to my school, though. He didn't even live in my town, so we hadn't seen each other since camp ended. But we'd written lots of letters and cards, and every now and then we spoke on the phone. Once, we had talked for an entire hour.

Was Will my boyfriend? I had thought I was in love with him when we were at camp. And I had to admit that I felt a funny thrill in my stomach every time I saw his return address on a letter. But that feeling was nothing compared to what I felt for Guy.

124

When I got back to the lodge, I couldn't help it: I raced up to our dormitory, found Stacey, pulled her into a corner, and said (not very quietly), "My ski instructor has a crush on me. His name is Guy, he's adorable, and he talks with an accent!"

"Oh, wow!" cried Stacey.

"Oh, wow!" cried Dawn. Then she added, "Sorry. I couldn't help overhearing."

"That's okay," I replied.

By dinnertime, all the BSC members, plus a few other friends, knew about Guy and me.

I didn't mind. I was proud of it.

14th CHAPTER

Jessi

Wednesday afternoon our team won the snow-sculpture contest! I am so excited. If the Red Team wins the snow-ball fight tomorrow, then we've won the war. It's too bad that Mal's and my snow-ballet slippers didn't win, but I think Claudia and Mr. Cheney liked them a lot. They stopped and looked at them for a long time and even whispered to each other about them. Oh, well.

After the contest was

over, I held auditions
for the talent show. It
is going to be so much fun,
and funny. Guess what—
the teachers want to do
a sketch of their own.
Of course, I have to
let them.

"Time's up!" called Kristy. "Everybody stop
what you're doing. The judging of the snow
sculpture contest is about to begin. Mr Cheney
and Claudia will be around to examine each
sculpture. Please stand with your hands behind
your backs."

"Oh, for pity's sake," muttered Mallory, and
giggled. She sounded exactly like her mother.

"Kristy loves rules. You know that," I said.
One thing I've learned is that everybody, even the
people you like best in the world, has faults, or
does things that annoy you. If you want to remain
friends with those people, then you choose to
overlook their faults. I overlook Kristy's bossiness
and love of rules. After all, she let me into her club
at a time when a lot of people in Stoneybrook
didn't like our family. Kristy's attitude was,
"Who cares? *I* like Jessi, we *all* like Jessi, she's a
good babysitter, so she stays." I've never forgotten
that about Kristy.

Anyway, I'm completely off the subject.

So Mal and I were standing like fools with our

hands behind our backs, waiting for Mr Cheney and Claud to evaluate the mammoth pair of snow ballet shoes we'd patted into shape. You could see the ribbons winding up the ankles and everything.

Next to our shoes three kids had built a massive snow castle (not too original when you consider that people on beaches always build sand castles). On our other side was a snow model of the Wicked Witch of the West from *The Wizard of Oz*. Claud and Mr Cheney walked from sculpture to sculpture, studying each one and whispering.

I watched them carefully. They stood for an awfully long time by one sculpture and when they moved away I saw that it was the Cheshire Cat from *Alice in Wonderland*—and that the kids who made it had tinted it with food colouring!

"Is that *fair*?" I explained to Mal.

"I suppose so," she replied. "Kristy didn't say we could *only* use snow. In fact, she didn't mention any rules except the time limit. And standing here with our hands behind our backs."

"Bother! Why weren't we more creative? Well, at least the Cheshire Cat's in our team."

After Claudia and Mr Cheney had consulted forever, the Cheshire Cat won. (Kristy looked as though she wanted to kill Claudia.) When the winner was announced, I made another announcement, reminding everyone about the auditions for the talent show, and then everyone who'd been sculpting on the lawn went off in different directions. Quite a few came to the grand ballroom to audition for the show.

Phew! Ever since I'd agreed to organize Talent Night a worry had been plaguing me: What if no one wanted to be in the show?

I should have known better. We're a lot of show-offs. I had even brought my *Swan Lake* costume with me and planned to dance a solo number. I'd decided that was my personal right as talent-show coordinator. (I also wanted to ensure that there would be at least one number in the show.)

"Okay, everybody," I shouted to the twenty or thirty kids who were milling around the ballroom. I stood up on the stage so they could hear me better. "Those of you who have pieces ready, stand on that side of the room," I said, pointing. "The rest of you stand on that side. I've got some ideas for you. Let me say in advance that the show is supposed to be forty-five minutes long, including the teachers' sketch, which they tell me is seven minutes, so we've got thirty-eight minutes— more or less—to work with. If we run slightly overtime, no one will kill us. But I want you to understand that I'll have to be a little choosey. Not everyone can be in the show or it'll be too long. I'm sorry, but that's what Miss Halliday told me, and she's the adviser for the talent show. Okay, let's begin with those of you who've prepared sketches or routines. I'll watch all of you and make my decision before you leave this afternoon."

Wow! As I stepped off the stage I felt quite proud of myself. The kids were really listening to me. Not only was I a lowly sixth-grader, but I was the only black sixth-grader at SMS—and for that reason the kids either used to ignore me or jeer at me. But that was some time ago, this was now. I was in charge, and everyone (even the eighth-graders) was listening.

"Okay, first number," I said. "Up on stage."

A seventh-grade girl, Davina, walked nervously on to the stage, sang some song called "Stop Pickin' on the President", and then played a couple of choruses on a harmonica with one hand while waving an American flag with the other.

I wrote her name on a notepad and put a big NO next to it.

The second act was Alan Gray and a friend of his, Rodge Somerset. They did a takeoff of a music-hall sketch. They were wearing top hats and carrying canes, and they told corny jokes like:

Alan: Hey, Rodge, did you get your hair cut?

Rodge: No, I got 'em *all* cut!

And, Alan: Did you hear about the fire down at the shoe factory?

Rodge: No, what happened?

Alan: A thousand soles were lost!

Their sketch was actually funny. I decided it was a possibility.

For the next hour, I watched act after act. A sixth-grade girl tap-danced to "Singin' in the Rain", wearing a raincoat and rain hat. Three seventh-grade boys did a tumbling act which was pretty good, and three seventh-grade girls dressed up as the Andrews Sisters and mimed to "Don't Sit Under the Apple Tree". An eighth-grade boy who announced himself as "The Flooglemeister" juggled three bananas while playing a kazoo and balancing a ski boot on his head. Then four girls put on a sketch that was a ghost story and both scary and funny. The last act I watched was a boy who could play all of "Doe, a Deer" with his armpit.

I studied my notes. Then I announced the acts

131

that I'd chosen for the show. I could see a lot of disappointed faces, so I added, "If your act wasn't selected, come and join the other group and you can audition for something else."

I was glad I'd organized the audition this way. You see, I knew there'd be some kids who were just dying to be in the show but really weren't that talented or didn't know what to do with themselves. I also knew that the teachers would be happy to see some nice normal acts in the show. So I had written a sketch about Leicester Lodge with lots of parts in it, and I had also arranged a simple song-and-dance routine to a fifties song that I like a lot called "Chains of Love".

When I had selected kids for those numbers and rehearsed each number twice, I sent Mal (who had volunteered to be my helper) off to find Mary Anne and the children from Conway Cove. She found them quickly—they'd been waiting eagerly for the ballroom to empty so they could get on with their part in the show—and they raced over to me.

"I know what I want to do! I know what I want to do!" the children were shouting. They were jumping up and down, except for Pinky, who was still supposed to be taking it easy on her foot.

"Okay, okay. One at a time," I said with a smile.

"Me first!" cried Joey. "Look at this. I can pretend I'm in a circus. See? First I'll pretend I'm a man on the flying trapeze. Then I'll be a bear on roller skates. Then I'll be a . . . *grrr* . . . lion tamer!" Joey proceeded to put on a one-man circus.

"My turn! My turn!" said Ginnie. "I can recite Shakespeare."

"*Shakespeare?!*" I couldn't help exclaiming.

"Yes. My big sister is in high school and she's in the drama club and she teaches me things all the time. Listen to this: 'A bee or not a bee. This is a question. If it's more noble to die, well, then I'll just have to die with my boots on.' "

I don't know much about Shakespeare, since we haven't studied any of his plays yet, but what Ginnie had said sounded . . . odd.

When Ginnie had finished, Amber wanted to do a four-legged tap dance. She said she could put tap shoes on her feet *and* her hands and dance to "How Much Is That Dog in the Window?" She also said that all four of her tap shoes were back in Conway Cove.

At this point I interrupted and said, "Mary Anne, I thought you were going to help the kids write a sketch. We don't have time for a million numbers—just one. What happened?"

Mary Anne shrugged. Her head had been in the clouds all week.

"Children," I said. "I hate to disappoint you, but we have time for just one number. I was thinking you could put on a sketch. Everyone could be in it."

"What kind of sketch?" said Pinky dubiously.

"Well . . ." I paused. The children would probably think a fairy tale would be too babyish. But maybe—"How would you like to put on a sketch about your school in Maine and your teachers? You know, *you* could be the teachers. You could be bossy and order people around and complain about the way children behave in the cafeteria."

The children's eyes lit up. A chance to get back at their teachers!

"Yes!" cried fifteen voices.

The sixteenth voice said, "No fear!" That was Pinky. "We'll get into trouble. Miss Weber and Mr Dougherty will see us!"

"Oh, they'll think it's funny," I said. "They'll understand."

"They won't."

"They *will*. So that's settled. We'll do a sketch about Conway Cove Elementary school."

The children cheered, except for Pinky, who narrowed her eyes at me. I narrowed mine back. Pinky was just going to have accept that black or not, I was in charge.

"She's so prejudiced," I said to Mal later.

But for once, Mal didn't agree with me. "I really don't think that's the problem this time," she told me.

But I knew better.

134

15th CHAPTER

Dawn

Thursday morning

I woke up in my bunk today feeling lower than low. It was awful knowing that Mary Anne was not in the top bunk, and furthermore, that she wasn't speaking to me. (Mary Anne, are you really going to put all this stuff in your book for Logan? Try to tone it down a little, okay? It's embarrassing.)

The day was grey as usual (has the sun shone once since we arrived?) and tonight the storm was supposed to hit. The big storm. Why didn't they

135

evacuate us? I suppose they thought we'd be safer if we stayed put than if we tried to travel home.

I hate having someone angry with me.

"Rise and shine!" called Kristy cheerfully from her bed. "Time to get up."

I sat up and hit my head on the bottom of Pinky's bunk.

"Hey!" she cried.

Claudia crawled sleepily out of her top bunk, stepping on Stacey's hand on the way down.

"Ow!" exclaimed Stacey.

Oh. So it was going to be one of *those* mornings.

My friends and I got dressed silently, except for occasional strained, polite conversation. Mary Anne and I were barely speaking, I was angry with Kristy, and Kristy and Claudia seemed pretty irritable, too. Only Mal and Jessi were acting normal. Even Stacey seemed a little funny —all daydreamy.

Mary Anne and I headed for the bathroom (after the boys had finished dressing), and reached the door at the same time.

"After you," I said coldly.

"Oh, no. After *you*." Mary Anne held the door open for me.

136

"Thank you very much."

"You're welcome!"

"Would you two calm down?" hissed Claudia, who was behind us. "You're making the children nervous. What's wrong with you, anyway?"

"Nothing," said Mary Anne and I at the same time.

Claudia raised her eyebrows. "Really?"

"Oh, all right. You forced me to say it. She's a pain," I said, pointing to Mary Anne.

"*I* am? What about you?"

"SHHH!" Claud closed the bathroom door, calling over her shoulder, "We'll be out in a minute. The bathroom's out of bounds." Then she looked at us. "Well?"

"Well, nothing," I said.

"Yes," agreed Mary Anne.

"Look, you two are best friends. Best friends do not call each other 'pains'." She paused.

Neither Mary Anne nor I said anything.

Claud sighed. "Okay, I suppose the fight isn't any of my business. But would you please try to be polite to each other in front of the children? They've been through a lot this week and they really look up to us."

"You're right," I agreed. "Okay."

"Yes," said Mary Anne.

So breakfast that morning went something like this:

Me: Mary Anne, could I please have the butter?

Mary Anne: Certainly. And enjoy it.

Me: Thank you *ever* so much.

Mary Anne: You are *ever* so welcome.

Kristy looked at us as if our heads were on back to front. Nevertheless, she was very business-like that morning. Shortly before breakfast ended, she stood up to make her usual morning announcement:

"The snowball fight will be held this afternoon from two till three. Remember, you can build forts and shelters, lay in supplies of ammunition—which means *snow*balls only, no slushballs—and the object of the fight is for one team to capture the other team's red or blue tennis ball that the team captains will have at the beginning of the fight, and which, by the way, must be hidden in the snow or a fort, *not* on a person.

"Please use the morning for ski practice or another practice snowball fight if you want to take part in the remaining events."

Kristy sat down, looking flushed, and Jessi immediately stood up.

"One more thing," she said. "We'll be rehearsing for Talent Night from ten to twelve in the grand ballroom this morning. Anyone in the show must be at rehearsal."

I felt like a real failure. I wasn't going to be in Jessi's show and I just couldn't bring myself to practise for the snowball fight or the ski competitions. Not after what had happened the day before.

And that wasn't like me. I'm not a quitter. I like to think I have a tough skin. After all, I survived my parents' messy marriage followed by their messy divorce, our move from California to Connecticut, my brother's move *back* to California, and the Trip-Man—that awful boyfriend Mum went out with before she began seeing Mary Anne's father seriously.

When breakfast was over, I hurried out of the dining hall, leaving the BSC members and the Conway Cove children behind. I just didn't feel like being with any of them. They all knew something was wrong and if they'd asked what it was, I was now so upset that I probably would have burst into tears and made a big scene.

Once I'd escaped from the dining room, though, I wasn't quite sure what to do with myself. I was about to make for the library to look for a book of ghost stories (my favourite way to escape) when someone tapped my arm and said, "Hey, Dawn!"

I turned around. It was Dori Wallingford, a girl I sometimes hang around with. "Hi," I said, trying not to look depressed.

"Hi," she replied. "Emily and I and a couple of other people here decided to play Monopoly all morning." (Dori's very grown up, but as unathletic as Mary Anne. She doesn't take part in the Winter War.) "Do you want to play? It's so yucky outside-—freezing cold and really windy. We're going to play at that table by the fireplace."

139

"Well . . . okay," I replied, thinking that it would be pretty hard to humiliate myself playing Monopoly. The only thing I could fall off was my chair, and that was unlikely.

True. But I soon found that there were other ways in which to humiliate myself—like landing in jail on practically every turn and then taking forever to get out. And consistently landing on the two properties on which Dori had built hotels. It wasn't long before I was entirely out of money.

"Gosh, I've never seen anyone lose so *fast*," said Dori.

I know she didn't intend to be mean, but her words unleashed something deep inside me. I had a feeling I was going to cry, so since I was

bankrupt anyway, I excused myself and made a run for the first-floor toilets. I hoped fervently that they'd be empty.

They weren't. Pinky was there. And *she* was crying. She was just sitting on the windowsill, her face in her hands, weeping as if her heart would break. When I saw her, I forgot all about needing to cry myself.

"Pinky!" I exclaimed. "What's wrong? Has something happened? Are you ill? Have you hurt your foot again?" (I was amazed at how much I sounded like my mother.)

"No," replied Pinky, sniffing. She wouldn't look at me, but she didn't seem angry, just sad.

"Are you lonely?" I asked.

Pinky shrugged.

"You can go out and play or skate or ski, you know. The doctor said it would be okay today."

"I know."

"Don't you want to?"

Pinky shrugged again.

I had an idea about what was wrong. Since I didn't want to embarrass Pinky, I said, "I'll tell you something. I feel a little like crying, too. And do you know why?"

Pinky finally looked at me. "Why?"

"Because I'm homesick."

"Really? You are? I think I am, too."

"Oh." I nodded.

"I've never been away from home before," said

141

Pinky in a rush. "But I've always been—what's the word? You know—I'm not afraid of anything. I go skateboarding, and I help my dad with his fishing business. I can steer the boat and I bring in lobster traps, too. I can do anything. But as soon as I got here, away from home, I felt like a baby. And now everyone has *seen* me act like a baby and I have to face my friends in school on Monday."

Well, that certainly explained a few things. Pinky was trying to cover up her fears by being too cool. Only she came over as bossy and snobby, as nasty and uncooperative. I'd seen the other children ignore her or leave her out. And I knew she'd been giving Jessi a hard time. Funny what being away from home can do to you.

And then I thought—maybe that's my problem, too. Oh, I'd been away from home plenty of times before. (And where was home, anyway? California? Connecticut? Both places?) But I wasn't used to being away with my whole school—with all the kids I'd have to see day in and day out for the rest of the year. When I came to Leicester Lodge in seventh grade, I'd just moved here and hardly anyone knew me, so I didn't care what the other kids thought of me. And when I went to Camp Mohawk, I knew I wouldn't see most of those kids again, except maybe for two weeks the following summer. But now if I made a fool of myself at the lodge, I'd have to live with it for the rest of the year.

Suddenly I leaned over and gave Pinky a hug. "Thank you," I said.

"For what?" Pinky actually smiled.

"For teaching me a lesson." It was something I was going to have to think about and deal with later—I wasn't as independent or as much of an individual as I'd thought. I would talk to Mum about it when I got home.

"Come on, Pinky," I said. "Let's go. I bet Curtis will make us some of his special hot chocolate."

16th CHAPTER

Mary Anne   Thursday

Dawn and I made up! I
can't believe it! I was so happy!
What an afternoon this was,
Logan. I wasn't in the
snowball fight, but a couple
of things happened. One of
them — you know what it
was, of course — was the best
part of the whole trip for me.
We are very busy getting
ready for the talent show
tonight, but all anyone can
talk about is the weather.
No snow is falling yet. But
it should start soon. Teensy
Mooseman has upgraded
her storm report from a
riproarer to a hurricane
I'm a little nervous....

I was so surprised at lunchtime today. The last I'd seen of Dawn was at breakfast, when we'd had daft conversations about passing the butter and that sort of thing. But when we met outside the dining hall at twelve-thirty, Dawn put her hand on my arm and said, "Mary Anne, let's talk, okay? Please?"

I almost said something really rude, but Dawn looked so earnest that I just replied, "Okay."

"We can go to our dormitory," Dawn went on. "I don't think anyone will be up there."

She was right.

Dawn sat on her bunk and patted the blanket beside her, so I sat next to her. "Mary Anne," she began, "I want to say that I'm really sorry about the way I've been acting. I think I know what got into me. And I know what got into you, too—Logan. You miss him, and I should have been more understanding. But what you didn't know was how I was feeling."

"How you were feeling?" I asked.

Dawn nodded. Then she told me about her conversation with Pinky.

"Oh, Dawn," I said, and I could feel my eyes filling with tears. Why do I have to cry over every little thing? "I should have been more sympathetic. I'm really sorry. All I could think about was Logan and me."

"Well, that's okay," Dawn replied, and *her* eyes filled with tears.

"No, it isn't." My tears spilled over.

"Yes, it is." Dawn's spilled over, too.

We were laughing and crying at the same time. Then I held my arms open and we hugged.

"Uh-oh," I said after a moment. "Lunch has started. We'd better go downstairs."

"Oh, we can be a few minutes late. There's something I have to do first."

"What?" I asked.

"This." Dawn ripped her blankets and sheets off the bunk under Pinky's and moved them under mine again. "There. Everything's back to normal. *Now* we can go to lunch."

So we did.

I was *so* glad that Dawn and I weren't fighting any more.

But soon lunch was over, the snowball fight had started (Dawn found the courage to join it, which made me very proud of her), and I found myself in the common room, alone with my book for Logan. I longed to talk to one of my friends, but Mal, Kristy, Dawn, and Claudia were in the fight; Jessi was in the grand ballroom with Miss Halliday, preparing for the show; and I didn't know where Stacey was. She'd been pretty scarce ever since Tuesday morning.

So I opened a notebook and started a letter to Logan, in Aruba:

146

My dearest, darling Logan,
 *How I miss you. How I
pine for you. How I yearn
and long for you.*
 *My life is not the same
without you. You are in my
every thought during the day,
and my every dream during the night.*

I paused. Maybe I was going a little overboard. I
didn't want Logan to think I wanted to marry him
or something. So I turned to a blank page and
started another letter:

Dear Logan,
 *I miss you. How is Aruba?
Leicester Lodge is fine. Having
a wonderful time. Wish you
were here.*

Well, that was pretty silly. That was the kind of
card you'd send when you'd gone to some charm-
ing tourist resort and were writing to someone
you barely knew, like an eighty-five-year-old
great-aunt who has blue hair and stuffs tissues up
her sleeves.

 I looked over my letters to Logan. I knew I
wasn't even going to send them, so I just sat and

thought. When I was finally able to drag my mind away from Logan, I mentally went over the sketch that the Conway Cove children were going to put on. I decided it would have to be changed. It was too . . . I don't know . . . babyish. And it was dated. It had been done a thousand times before. The children should do something really original.

I put my pen in my mouth. Then I took it out and began scribbling ideas for a new sketch. It was all about a girl who was breaking up with her boyfriend. Kara, who was sophisticated for her age, and also one of the older girls, would be perfect for the female lead. She was a bit of a feminist anyway, so she'd be likely to get angry if she thought her boyfriend treated her unfairly. And Ian, who had strict ideas about what boys and girls can and can't do, would be great for Kara's chauvinist boyfriend.

I wrote and wrote and wrote. When I thought the play was pretty polished, I ran into the grand ballroom with it.

"Jessi!" I called.

Jessi was collecting props with Miss Halliday, but she ran over to me.

"Hi!" she said. "What's the matter?"

"I've rewritten the sketch for the children. I think it'll be much more appealing to the audience. What do you think?"

Jessi took the script from me and read it in silence. She pursed her lips. Then she put her hand over her mouth. I could see her dimples, though, which meant she was smiling. But when she took her hand away she looked like the ordinary Jessi.

"Um, Mary Anne," she began, "this sketch is—is good. Honestly, it is. But I'm not sure it's right for the children. Besides, they love the idea of making fun of their teachers, and anyway, they've already learned the first sketch. They don't have time to learn a new one. The talent show will be just a few hours from how."

"You're right. I didn't think of that," I replied, feeling a little foolish. "Sorry I interrupted you."

"Don't worry. I'm glad you're so interested in the show."

"Is there anything I can do to help you?" I asked.

Jessi looked thoughtful. "Nothing now," she answered after a moment. "But I'll need you at rehearsal."

"Okay," I replied.

I wandered back out to the common room and sat down with my notebook. I looked over the information I'd gathered on the lodge and Hooksett Crossing. I actually had a fair amount. I'd be able to write the essay without any trouble as soon as I got home.

So I began yet another letter to Logan. I had got as far as, "Dear Logan, light of my life," when a man behind the reception desk said loudly, "Is there a Mary Anne Spier here? A Mary Anne Spier?"

I stood up, startled. "I'm Mary Anne Spier," I told him.

"Oh, good. I tried your dormitory and there was no answer, so I'd thought I'd page you. I'm glad you're here. I've got a long-distance phone-call for you."

A long distance call? For *me*?" I was amazed. As far as I knew, no other kid from SMS had got a call here except for dopey Alvin Hopper. His mother had phoned to make sure he was taking his allergy pills. No one could believe it. I hated to be put in the same category as wheezy Alvin.

But then something occurred to me. A long-distance call could only be from one person—my father. And he wouldn't phone unless there was an emergency. Right away, I was sure something was wrong. My mind began racing:

Dad had had a heart attack and was in hospital.

Dad had been in a car accident.

Our house had burned down.

Tigger had been hit by a car.

I wished Dawn were there to hold my hand while I took the call, but I knew I would have to be brave and handle the situation myself.

I took the phone gingerly from the desk clerk and faced a corner so no one would see me when I started to cry.

150

"Hello, Dad?" I said.

"Mary Anne?" ventured the voice on the other end of the line. "This is Logan."

"LOGAN?" I screeched. Then I remembered where I was and lowered my voice. "Logan! Where are you? I can't believe it's you!"

"Well, it is. And I'm down here in Aruba. How are you? I've been thinking about you day and night."

"Oh, me too. I mean, *I've* been thinking about *you*. How's Aruba?"

"Fine, but I miss you."

"You do?"

"Of course. Don't you miss me?"

"Oh, *yes*. I can't tell you how much. What are you doing? What's the weather like? Have you met any nice gi— any nice people?"

"A few. There's a family from Piscataway, New Jersey, in the room next to ours. They have a girl—"

"A *girl?*" I gasped.

"—of exactly Hunter's age."

I sighed with relief. Hunter is Logan's little brother.

"What's going on at the lodge?" Logan continued. "I'm having fun here, but I rather wish I were with all of you in Vermont."

"Oh, Logan, you won't believe what's happened this week." I told him about the two bus accidents and the children from Maine. I told him about my fight with Dawn, about Claudia and Kristy's ski war, and about the talent show, "*And*," I went on, "we're supposed to get a *huge* storm here tonight. We might even get snowed in."

"Well, don't get snowed in past Sunday. I'll die if I can't see you when I come home."

"You will?" I said in a small voice.

"Figuratively speaking."

"Oh, Logan. I love you."

"I love you, too, Mary Anne."

I hung up the phone, feeling like a new person.

17th CHAPTER

Mallory

Thursday evening

The storm hit at exactly six-fifteen tonight, right in the middle of dinner. The snowball fight had ended in howling wind and freezing temperatures. (The Blue Team won, as you know, Mary Anne, so Kristy is overjoyed, certain that now her team will win the Winter War.) Anyway, in the middle of dinner, someone cried, "Hey, it's snowing!" and sure enough, it was. Tiny flakes were falling thickly and furiously. I don't want to be snowed in unless we can be evacuated tomorrow.

By the way, my journal project is not going too well.

153

Mallory

Not going too well? My diary was a failure, unless you consider learning from big mistakes to be a success. But I didn't want to admit that to Mary Anne or any of my friends. Two things had gone wrong. One, I'd been caught spying a couple of times. Two, hardly anything that I thought I'd observed had actually happened.

For starters, the cook (whose name I found out is Curtis) is probably not crazy. Anyway, he isn't trying to poison us all. If he were, somebody would be dead by now, but everyone's fine, all bodies are accounted for. I sneaked into the kitchen to try to find out what it was I'd seen Curtis sprinkling into the food, but Curtis sneaked up on *me* and nearly scared me to death.

The powder was probably garlic or parmesan cheese. Sometimes people keep them in unlabelled jars.

Then, just this morning, I was tiptoeing around the lodge with my diary and I came across Stacey and this boy Pierre she's been spending so much time with. I passed by the doorway to the library and they were in there alone, sitting very close together on a sofa. I thought that maybe if I stood outside and peeped at them through the crack in the door, I could find out just what goes on when a boy and a girl kiss. (I've been *dying* to know.) But I hadn't been there long when Pierre said softly to Stacey, "Either I'm crazy or that door has eyes."

Stacey was off the couch and in the hall in a flash. She caught me red-handed!

"Mallory!" she exclaimed. "What are you doing?"

"Nothing," I replied, which is the best answer to give when you know you're doing something that someone will disapprove of.

"Are you sure?"

"Positive," I replied, trying to hide my diary. I escaped in a hurry.

The last thing that happened was the one that convinced me I knew nothing at all about observational skills. I didn't need to sharpen them. I needed to *acquire* them. Remember when I saw Miss Halliday crying in the bathroom and decided

it was because she was in love with the deputy head (don't worry, he's not married or anything), but that he didn't love her back? Well, later I overheard her talking to Mary Anne and it turns out she's engaged to someone in Stoneybrook and she was just upset because she missed him.

Maybe, I decided, spying was not the best method of gathering information. Or if it was, I'd have to learn how to do it without reading all sorts of things into what I saw and letting my imagination run away with me. Like Jessi. She decided that Pinky's nasty behaviour was a result of being prejudiced. But if Jessi had opened her eyes and looked beyond her own problems, she'd have seen that Pinky was having some trouble being away from home. And furthermore, that she was being unpleasant to everyone, not just Jessi.

Anyway, back to Thursday evening. That night was a big one. Not only had the storm hit, but it was Talent Night and Jessi was in a frenzy. Also, before the show began, all of us were to gather in the common room, where a roaring fire was going, and where we were going to be served Curtis's famous hot chocolate. (I was glad I didn't need to worry about his poisoning us any more.)

While we drank the hot chocolate, we were going to tell ghost stories! I was afraid that the Conway Cove children, who were invited since

they were going to be in the show later, would be
too scared, but they insisted on coming.

"I know they're going to have bad dreams all
night. I just know it," I told Jessi.

But Jessi was too busy worrying about the show
to answer me.

At seven o'clock, we gathered in the common
room. Now, that room is big, but I have to admit
that seating the sixth-graders, seventh-graders,
eighth-graders, and the Conway Cove children,
the SMS teachers, the Georges, and Curtis (who
was pouring out his hot chocolate) was a bit
crowded. We were jammed all over the floor, the
sofas, and the chairs. But I felt cosy and excited
with the storm whistling and blowing outside.

When the hot chocolate had been served, Mr
Cheney stood up and said, "Attention, and
welcome to the ghostly portion of Talent Night."
(Everyone laughed.) "We'll be telling our scariest
stories for the next hour, and then we'll move to
the grand ballroom for the show. By the way, the
teachers are going to tell their stories first. That's
one of the prerogatives of being a teacher."
(Sometimes Mr Cheney likes to impress us pupils
with big words. In case you don't know what
"prerogative" means—and I didn't—it's a special
right or privilege.) "Anyone who wants to tell a
story," Mr Cheney went on, "just put up your
hand and come and stand in front of the fire so the
others can see and hear you."

157

At that point the lights dimmed, and Mr
Cheney himself walked to the fireplace. The room
grew quiet. All around me, kids leaned forward
slightly.

"My story," Mr Cheney began in a low, spooky
voice, the firelight flickering behind him with an
eerie glow, "takes place in a nice, normal neighbourhood. It could be your neighbourhood in
Stoneybrook." (I shivered.) "On Silver Fox Lane
lived a young woman. She wasn't married, but
she had a good job and had just bought a house
that she loved. However, she'd always been
nervous about living alone, so she also bought a
big guard dog, Butch, to protect her.

"One night, the woman came home and found
the front door of her house open. Straight away,
she became scared. She knew someone had
broken in.

" 'Butch!' she called. 'Butch?'

"She didn't hear a sound, so she flicked on the
light in the hall. She saw blood everywhere—but
nothing seemed to be missing. She could see her
TV and her stereo in the living room.

"Now the woman was clever and knew she
should get out of her house and call the police, so
she did. When they arrived, they searched everywhere. The only unusual thing they found, apart
from the blood, was Butch lying unconscious on
the kitchen floor. The woman screamed. Then
she rushed Butch to the vet, and the vet performed

emergency surgery. And do you know what he found in Butch's stomach? . . . A man's finger. Butch had torn it off the intruder when he broke into the house, and had accidentally swallowed it.''

All around me kids were gasping.

"Oh, yuck," I said to Jessi. "That's so disgusting. Do you think it's true?"

Jessi looked at me wide-eyed. "It could be," she whispered. And she really jumped when, right then, Pinky scrambled into her lap for safety.

We hardly had time to think about Pinky, though, because as soon as Mr Cheney had returned to his seat on the sofa, Miss Halliday stood up.

"My story," she began, "is about a man and wife who were on their honeymoon. They were driving along a deserted road very late at night, listening to the radio. Suddenly an old Beatles song was interrupted by a newsflash. 'We have just learned,' said the announcer, 'that an insane murderer has escaped from the Towson County Jail. Please do not go out alone, and keep all your doors and windows locked. Thank you.'

"Well, the couple was scared to death. And wouldn't you know, just as the announcement ended, one of their tyres burst, so the man left the woman alone in the car while he went looking for a garage. He'd been gone for about fifteen minutes when the woman started to hear a faint

159

scratching sound, like this—*scritch-scratch—scritch-scratch*—on the roof of the car."

At that moment, every light in the lodge went out.

"Aaghhh!" we screamed. Even the eighth-grade boys screamed.

Jessi tried to grab me, but Pinky was hugging her too tightly.

"He's here! He's here!" someone cried. "It's the insane murderer!"

"No, it's the Leicester Lodge ghost!" exclaimed Curtis.

"Hey, hey, hey!" I recognized Mr George's voice. "Hold your horses. The power's gone out, that's all. It happens nearly every time we have a big storm. Just sit tight and I'll turn on the emergency generator."

The room grew silent. I watched a torch bob away, the figure of Mr George behind it.

"Shall I continue my story?" asked Miss Halliday.

"NO!" we screeched.

A few more silent moments passed. They seemed like weeks. Then Pinky said in a whisper that was almost a sob, "We're going to get snowed in, aren't we? We're going to get stuck here. We'll never be able to go home, and the insane murderer will kill us all."

"Maybe they'll evacuate us tomorrow," Jessi said uncertainly to me.

Evacuate us tomorrow? Really? If that happened, there would be no all-school dance. I wouldn't have to go! Despite the storm and the power failure, I began to feel a little better. I prayed for a gigantic storm and an evacuation.

But Mr George spoiled it all. The lights came back on, and a few minutes later he reappeared saying, "Good news. I just heard the weather report. Now they're saying that the storm is supposed to pass to the east of us. The worst is probably over. When you wake up tomorrow, you'll find sunshine and about ten centimetres of fresh snow for your ski competitions."

BOTHER!

No blizzard and the dance would be held after all. And there didn't seem to be any sign of the ghost Mary Anne had told us about. I supposed the "ghost" was just another ghost story.

Miss Halliday finished her story. "So, anyway," she said, "the woman waited all night for her husband to come back. He never did. But the woman heard the scratching noises until the next morning, when a police car pulled up alongside her.

" 'Stay in the car, madam!' shouted a police officer.

"The woman followed his instructions. There was a huge scuffle, and a man was pulled off the roof of her car, handcuffed, and led to the squad car. It was the insane murderer! He had killed her

161

husband, and was after the woman. All night he had lain on the roof of her car where she couldn't see him, and had been scratching through it with his *fingernails*. Another eighth of an inch and he would have killed the woman, too!"

I nearly fainted. Then two more teachers told us tales that scared us to death. After that, the kids started telling stories. We heard about ghostly hitchhikers, about campers who were the prey of escaped convicts, about some more honeymoon couples, and we heard one particularly scary story that Stacey's friend Pierre told, called "Three-Fingered Billy".

But I only half heard them. I couldn't stop thinking about the dance the next night. I knew I was going to make a fool of myself.

18th CHAPTER

Jessi

Thursday night

Hi, Mary Anne. Well,
you were there. You
were at the talent
show. So you know
what went on. Anyway,
this is mean, but
I just couldn't help
laughing (to myself) when
Dimples got mixed up
during her sketch. You
have to admit it was
funny. I also couldn't
help feeling very proud
after my own sketch.
What you don't know
about is what happened
after the show. It

163

happened between Pinky and me, and part of it was really nice, but the rest of it sure gave me something to think about. I'll have to talk to Mama and Daddy when I get home. Becca, too. I think we should call a family conference. I know I need one.

Oh, golly. Was I nervous before the show began! I had never been in charge of something as big as Talent Night. And I was going to be *in* the show too. I thought that was fair. Besides, there were a few kids that I needed to show off in front of. But I had to be sure to do a good job.

When the scary stories were over and the hot chocolate finished, we all moved into the grand ballroom. It had been set up like a theatre. There was the stage with a curtain at one end of the room, and now row after row of folding chairs had been set up so that everyone would have a place to sit down.

While the audience settled into the chairs, I ran backstage with the kids who were going to be performing. I quickly counted heads. Everyone was present.

"Okay," I said, "I think you know the order in which you're supposed to go on stage, but in case you forget, I've pinned up a list in the wings. Remember, the teachers go first, the Conway Cove children go last, and when the show is over, we all run on stage in two lines, holding hands, for the curtain call.

"Now all the props are over there," (I pointed to a sturdy folding table) "and Callie is in charge of the music. If you need music for your number, just hand her your tape before you go on stage and she'll put it in the tape deck. Any questions?"

There weren't, so I tapped Terry Morgan on the arm and said, "You're on, Mr Announcer."

As coordinator of the show, I suppose I could have been the announcer, but when Terry's plan to dress up like Father Goose and recite nursery rhymes in Italian wasn't accepted by me as an act for the show, he begged to do something—*any*thing. So I told him he could be the announcer. (Besides, I would have felt funny announcing myself later on.)

When I felt that the kids were ready to begin the show, I signalled to Miss Halliday, who signalled to someone else, and the lights in the grand ballroom were dimmed, except for two bright ones on the stage.

I nodded to Terry, he nodded back, and then he stepped confidently on to the stage. "Good evening, ladies and germs," he began. (I had told him he could say that.) "Well, I just flew in from Stoneybrook and, gosh, are my arms tired!" (The audience groaned, but they were laughing, too.) "Anyway, welcome to Talent Night. We in the show have enjoyed preparing these numbers for you, and we hope you will enjoy seeing them. And now without further adieu," (I had *not* told Terry he could say that) "may I present the SMSTs."

Terry walked offstage in one direction while the SMS teachers walked on from the opposite direction. There were eight of them, and they were all wearing red polo-neck sweaters and jeans, and carrying microphones.

One teacher stepped forward, and said, "Welcome to the Do-wop Stop". Then he stepped back in line. For the next seven or so minutes those teachers sang a medley of fifties hits. That in itself was pretty good because it turned out that these maths and social studies teachers could actually harmonize. But the fun part was that they'd changed the words of the songs, so they were singing about things like kids skipping classes, the noise in the cafeteria, the bus ride to Leicester Lodge, and even the Winter War. When they had finished, they somehow seemed like real people to me, instead of just teachers. I suppose they sounded like that to the rest of the kids, too, because they got a huge round of applause.

The next act was Dimples Howard (that was her stage name, of course), doing her tap number to "Singin' in the Rain". Terry introduced her as the Titan of Tap, but I don't think anyone knew what he meant.

"Wait till I reach the middle of the stage before you start the music," Dimples told Callie as she handed her the cassette.

"Okay," said Callie.

Then Dimples, who was already wearing her raincoat, tied on a rain bonnet and stooped down to buckle one of her shoes. But the buckle broke and it took her so long to fix it that the audience got restless and Callie started the tape, just so people would have something to listen to. By the time Dimples ran onstage, the audience was listening to the end of the second verse of her song and Dimples couldn't find her place.

"Start it again!" she hissed to Callie, but Callie got flustered and fast-forwarded to some later spot in the song, so Dimples just sort of improvised until the song was over. When that happened, Dimples stayed onstage and demonstrated the single, double, and triple time steps as well as the Manhattan time step, so at least she felt she had shown what she was capable of doing.

The next act was a personal favourite of mine, partly because it involved no music. Bobby Henson, who had wanted to play "Doe, a Deer" with his armpit, which I wouldn't let him do, then decided to dress up as Lucille Ball and imitate her rehearsing a TV advertisement for a product

called Vitameatavegamin, which he assured me
happened during an *I Love Lucy* show entitled
"Lucy does a TV advertisement".

"Hello, friends," Bobby began. (He was wearing a polka-dotted dress, and a lady's hat and
gloves, which was pretty funny for a start, so
already kids were laughing.) "Are you tired, run-
down, listless? Are you unpopular?"

Bobby had memorized the whole advertisement
—including the way Lucy started getting it
wrong. I saw one kid in the audience laugh so
hard that he began coughing and had to leave the
grand ballroom for a drink of water.

The show continued. The Flooglemeister was a
big hit, despite the fact that Terry introduced him
as the Frugalmaster. The girls who imitated the
Andrews Sisters were a hit, too. Then came the
funny ghost story, the sketch about Leicester
Lodge, the "Chains of Love" number, and finally
. . . my dance routine. After so much hilarity, I
hoped the kids were ready for me because *Swan
Lake* was serious, not funny.

The kids *were* ready. Even so, I was nervous,
but I've danced in front of big audiences before,
and I know how to ignore the audience and pay
attention only to the music and the movements of
my body. So I turned and pirouetted in a world of
my own, not returning to the real world until the
music was over.

When I stopped dancing, there was a moment

of silence. Then the kids and teachers, even the ones backstage, began clapping loudly. A few kids even whistled! I felt as if I had *finally, really* been accepted at Stoneybrook Middle School, which was why I grinned until my face nearly fell off.

The last act of the evening was the sketch formed by the Conway Cove children. They were looking a little tired from the excitement of the evening—the snowstorm, the power failure, the ghost stories, and the talent show—but they pulled themselves together nicely. When I gave them the cue, they ran out on the stage, introduced the characters they would be playing, and launched right into the sketch. Not one of them forgot a line, and they spoke clearly and confidently, even

169

Pinky, and thank goodness, because she had one of the funniest parts. She played a teacher named Miss Wyndham, who I gathered had been at their school for decades, and whose claim to fame was that she'd once got a grape stuck up her nose. Personally, I thought it was one of those stories that had never happened but was destined to circulate the school each year for as long as Miss Wyndham continued to teach. At any rate, Pinky got tons of laughs.

So I was quite surprised to find her crying in the first-floor bathroom after the show. I'd gone in there to be by myself for a few minutes before tackling the job of helping my friends put the children to bed. I just needed some of what Mama calls "cooling down time".

But there was Pinky sobbing over one of the basins.

"Pinky! What's the matter?" I exclaimed. "Why are you crying? Your sketch went perfectly. Everyone loved it. They especially loved you."

Pinky shook her head. "It's not that."

"It isn't? What's wrong?"

Pinky paused. Finally she said, "Just homesick, I suppose." Then she added, "I know I was really unkind to you this week, Jessi. I'm sorry."

I was so surprised that I didn't know what to say. Pinky must have thought I was angry, because she rushed on, "I've been unkind to everyone, and I know it. I'm *really* sorry." She looked pleadingly at me.

"Oh, Pinky," I said. "That's okay. I mean, I did think you didn't like me, but I'm not angry. Not any more."

Pinky began talking to me again, but I had some difficulty paying attention to her. I was remembering something that Mallory had said to me, something about Pinky's not being prejudiced. And I was remembering Pinky bossing the other children around and the children then excluding her from things.

Why was it that I had overlooked all that and focused on what Pinky had said and done only to me (like ordering me to get her a drink)? Was it because of the bad experiences I'd had in Stoneybrook with our neighbours? Probably. But did that mean *I* was prejudiced in some way now? I hoped not. But I knew I would need to have a long talk with my parents when I got back from Leicester Lodge.

"Come on, Pinky," I said, holding my hand out to her. "It's late. We should go to bed."

Pinky sighed softly. "Okay," she replied.

Hand in hand, we went upstairs to our dormitory.

19th CHAPTER

Claudia

Firday morning
Mr Goerge said
the snowstrom would pass us
bye and he was wright. Well it
didn't excatly pass us by but we
only got three inchis Im not complaning
though. This is prefect for the ski
compertitons which are downhill this
monring and x- county this afternon.
I'am pretty sure the red Team will
wine!

Guess waht. The sun is shinning
for the frist time today. Its a
good thing I broght along my new
ski gogles. They will be handy. More
improtant Gu Guy (Stasey helped
me speel that) will be impresed I
think.

The skiing competitions! I'd been waiting for them all week. For me, they would be the highlight of the trip. They always are, especially downhill. And this time, Guy would be there to cheer me along. He had promised on Thursday after giving me a private lesson. Note that I said *private*. How that happened was that on Thursday morning after I took a class with him I said, "Will you be teaching another class late this afternoon? The skiing competitions are tomorrow and I could do with some extra help."

What do you think Guy said? He said, "No, I do not have a class scheduled, bot for you I weel make an exception. How about a priveet lesson at sree-sirty?"

Sree-sirty? Oh, three-thirty.

"Of course," I replied.

So I had a private lesson with Guy. He was very helpful. But I have to say that I was having just a little trouble concentrating. At one point he positioned my body for the perfect ski stance. As soon as his mittens touched my parka, my mind went into orbit. It was flying around in outer space. All I could think of was Guy and me sitting in a darkened restaurant together. The maitre d' has given us a quiet, intimate table in the back with a candle in a glass holder in the middle of the table. By the flickering light, Guy takes my hand in his and says—

173

"Zat eez very goode. You are ready for your ron now."

No, no. That wasn't what he said in the daydream. That was what he said during the lesson.

I let myself fly. Down the mountain I went. And off into outerspace went my mind again. This time, Guy and I are walking along a beach at sunset. In that light, the sand looks pink. To our right are palm trees with fat coconuts hanging from them. To our left is the ocean reflecting the setting sun. Guy and I are holding hands. We're laughing. We're—

Coming to the bottom of the mountain! I put on the brakes, but I knew the end of my run had been sloppy. Guy confirmed that when I got off the ski lift.

"If you want to be zee best tomorrow," he said, "you must not let your mind wander. Do you onderstand? You deed well, bot you can do moch better."

I nodded and took another run, this time allowing myself only a brief fantasy about sitting in a boat on a canal in Venice with Guy before dragging my mind back to skiing. I was later rewarded with an ear-to-ear grin from Guy and a pat on the back. Or was it a small hug? I couldn't be sure.

Anyway, by Friday morning I knew I was ready

for the downhill skiing competition. It would be my best event, and I was pretty sure I could win it for my team. This is how the competition would work: The members of each team had been put into a beginners group, an intermediate group, or an advanced group. (That was so beginners could be in the event without having to compete against experts. By the way, Kristy and I were in the advanced groups on our teams. Dawn was in an intermediate group, and Stacey asked to be in a beginners group, although I think she could have competed with the intermediates.)

Each kid in each group, starting with the advanced skiers, would take a run downhill. They would be judged on both speed and performance by the head ski instructor at the lodge. The winning beginner would earn five points for his or her team, the winning intermediate seven points, and the winning advanced skier nine points. Therefore it was possible for one team to beat the other by winning all three categories, or for a race to be as close as one team earning nine points and the other twelve.

At breakfast on Friday, Kristy was impossible. "We're going to beat the pants off you lot," she said to me. "And then we'll beat you in cross-country so we'll have *won* the *war!*" She looked jubilant at the very thought.

"Big deal," I replied. "So you'll each get a

piece of pizza. We've got frozen pizza at our house all the time. I can have it whenever I want."

"You know that's not what I mean," said Kristy.

"Yes, all you think about is winning," I told her sarcastically.

"That's right." Kristy stuffed a piece of toast in her mouth. "Ishm mat the pot?"

"What?" I said.

Kristy swallowed. "Isn't that the point?"

Before the discussion could get any more unpleasant, Mal changed the subject. She turned to Pinky and the other children. "Who wants to go ice-skating this morning?" she asked.

"Me! I do!" cried most of them—including Pinky.

"You'd better start getting them dressed as *soon* as breakfast is over," Stacey whispered to Mal. "It could take hours to get them ready."

Not much later, the downhill skiing competition was about to begin. The advanced skiers had gathered at the top of the nearest mountain, the intermediates were further down, and the beginners were at the head of one of the nursery slopes. A big crowd of people was waiting at the bottom of the mountain. This Winter War event got more attention than any other, so we had a pretty good audience.

The most important member of the audience for me, however, was . . . Guy, of course. And *he*

176

wasn't just milling around with the crowd below. *He* was standing at the top, still giving me hints and an occasional pat on the back. (Hug?)

The advanced skiers were to take their runs first, and everyone knew that the real competition would be between Kristy and me, since each of us was the best skier in our respective teams.

The event began. The lodge's head skiing instructor, Miss Olsen, tossed a coin. My team were heads—and we won the toss. Rick chose Lindsay McManus to lead, and off she went. She was good, and reached the bottom with a fast time. The next skier was Miranda Elliot from Kristy's team. She was even better and faster.

One after another the advanced skiers whipped

177

down the slope. Finally, only Kristy and I were left. Kristy poised herself at the top of the run. I could almost see her gathering her concentration and shutting out everything but the slope and her skis.

Kristy earned the fastest time yet. When she heard the news she let out a yell. "All *right!* The Blue Team is bound to win now!"

I'll admit it, she was winding me up. But just before I poised myself for my run, Guy touched my arm and whispered in my ear, "Concentrate."

I concentrated.

I also beat Kristy. I had earned nine points for our team. "You're wrong, Thomas!" I cried. "The *Red* Team is bound to win now!"

But as it turned out, I was wrong. I couldn't believe it. The Blue Team won in both the intermediate and the beginners' competitions. They beat us twelve to nine.

"We've tied! We've tied!" Kristy shouted. "And the Blue Team is going to beat the Red Team in cross-country."

"How?" asked Rick. "Hardly anyone entered the event in your team. We've got all the good cross-country skiers."

"No you haven't," replied Kristy, which is a way of letting people know that suddenly you're not sure of yourself.

I looked at my watch. Lunchtime—and I was starved. The SMS kids made their way into the dining hall to fuel up before the last event of the Winter War. Although we had lost in downhill skiing, I felt as though I was walking on air.

"Guy really likes me," I told the BSC members as we ate our lunch.

"But he's too old for you," said Mary Anne.

"Age doesn't matter," I replied, trying to sound as wise as my grandmother Mimi would have sounded if she'd still been alive.

"How can you be sure he really likes you?" asked Jessi.

"Oh, just by the way he looks at me. By the way he gives me encouragement, pats me on the back, wants to spend time with—"

I stopped talking. My eyeballs almost shot out of their sockets. I had looked away from Jessi and seen Guy approaching me. He was carrying a baby in one arm, a little girl was holding his free hand, and a beautiful woman was with him.

"Hello," said Guy. "Claudia, I wanted you to meet my family. Zees baby here eez Jean, zees leetle won eez my daughter, Marie, and zees eez my wife, Domitille. Domi, zees eez Claudia, zee wonderful skier I woz telling you about."

I don't know how I got through that conversation, but I did. I even managed to smile. When Guy and his family left, our table was silent. No one said a word, not even Kristy. In fact, she put her arm around me for a moment.

I tried to tell myself it would never have

179

worked out anyway. He really *is* too old. And then I thought, Thank goodness for Will. I've still got Will.

But my feelings had been wounded.

20th CHAPTER

Kristy

Friday afternoon

The cross-country skiing event was held this afternoon, Mary Anne. You didn't see it since the Conway Cove kids wanted to go sledging on the lawn in front of the lodge and you agreed to watch them after Mrs George gave the kids her permission. So you weren't around for what happened during the final event of the Winter War, although I'm sure you heard about it. It all began when I got carried away with myself at lunchtime....

Kristy

I wish I'd had a camera with me in the dining hall so I could have captured the look on Claud's face when Guy walked over to her with his wife and kids. No, I don't wish that at all. It would have been mean. Claud's feelings were *really* hurt. I think I'll remember the look on her face even without a camera.

And although I honestly did feel sorry for Claudia, I suppose I'm slightly mean (maybe everyone is, I don't know), because some teeny-tiny part of me couldn't help thinking, "If Claud is upset, maybe she won't do well in cross-country skiing this afternoon and her team will lose." Isn't that awful? But that's how I felt. I just wanted to win so *badly*. And the Blue Team was so *close*.

That was only the beginning of how I went win-crazy that afternoon, though. Next, I waited until Claudia had composed herself, and kids were starting to finish their lunches, before I tapped on my glass to make an announcement.

"Attention, Blue Team members!" I said. "Attention, please! As you know, this afternoon is our last chance to beat the Red Team. As you may *not* know, we don't have nearly enough good cross-country skiers signed up for this event. Come on, all of you! It's not too late to join the team. How many of you out there are willing to join so we can win the war?"

I thought I sounded like a coach giving his

team a good pep talk, but instead of enthusiastic shouts, I just heard some murmurs and saw a couple of heads nod.

Cross-country skiing isn't the most popular event to enter.

Oh, well. Desperate times call for desperate measures.

So first I asked Dawn to take part in the event. I received a definite no. She'd got through the snowball fight and downhill skiing (doing well, by the way), but wasn't about to risk trying a new sport. So I began walking from table to table. At each one I personally asked the Blue Team members to join the final event of the war.

"Anyone can cross-country ski," I said to Shawn Benedict. "Have you used ordinary skis?"

Shawn shook her head.

"Oh. Well, that doesn't matter," I went on. "If you can walk, you can cross-country ski. So join up, okay? We *really need* you."

"All right," said Shawn uncertainly. "If you promise it's that easy."

"I promise," I told her. I looked at Jay Marsden, who was sitting opposite Shawn. "What about you? If you can walk, you—"

"I know, I know. If I can walk, I can ski," he said.

"So?"

"Gosh, I don't know, Kristy."

"Come *on*. For our team. For the war. Where's your team spirit?"

Jay looked embarrassed. "All right. I'll join."

"Great!"

I approached another table, but the kids there must have overheard my conversations with Shawn and Jay because before I could even open my mouth, three of them said, "We can't walk yet!"

"Spoilsports," I muttered as I headed for the next table. There I talked two more kids into entering the event. By the time lunch was over, the Blue Team had gained thirteen new contestants in cross-country skiing. Now we had twenty-eight contestants and Rick's team had twenty.

Since there was a full hour before the competition was to begin, I took all the novice skiers to the hire shop, helped get them fitted with cross-country skis, and gave them a fast lesson. I'm not much of a cross-country skier myself, but I thought I knew more than they did. Besides, all they'd be asked to do in the event was ski a short trail.

This is how the competition would work: Groups of four kids—two from my team, two from Rick's—would ski similar-length trails at the same time. The kid who crossed the finishing line first would score a point for his or her team. Since Rick's team now had fewer members than mine, some of his skiers would go twice. Rick would pick the best ones, of course . . . if they weren't too tired. I had a feeling that sheer numbers would make up for talent.

Our practice hour was, well, let's just say it wasn't ideal. Shawn couldn't stay up on her skis. I've never seen one person fall down so often in such a short period of time. She'd be up on her feet, then BOOM! in the snow, up on her feet, then BOOM! in the snow.

"Kristy," she said at last, "in case you're interested, I'm not enjoying myself."

"Just try *one more time*," I begged her.

Shawn struggled to her feet. Her face was scarlet. But at least she stayed up. She seemed to be getting the hang of things.

Before I knew it, the hour was up and it was time for the competition to begin.

"Kristy," Jay said to me nervously, "I can stay on my feet all right, but I really can't go very fast. I've got a bad feeling about this."

"Don't worry," I told him. "No one's much good at this event. Honestly."

I was half right. No one on *my* team seemed to be much good. At least not in the beginning. I hoped, though, that was because I was sending my most inexperienced team members out first, so they could get things over with and we would catch up later.

We lost race after race.

The lodge's cross-country ski instructor would stand by the queue of kids who were competing in each round, shout, "On your marks, get set, GO!" and *my* team members would barely get themselves moving while the other two kids would be halfway to the finishing line.

I put Shawn in the first race so she could stop looking so uncomfortable. Suddenly, she seemed to be back in our practice session. The instructor shouted, "GO!" and immediately Shawn was sitting on her bottom. I felt pretty sorry for her, especially when a few kids around us started sniggering. Poor Shawn didn't even try to catch up with the others. She just took off her skis and watched Rick's team win the race.

I put Jay in the fourth round. He actually skied about three-quarters of the way to the finish before he fell. But when he landed we all heard the *snap* and his agonized cry.

"Oh!" he shouted. "Help! I think I've broken something."

In the blink of an eye, two teachers and the lodge doctor raced to Jay. The doctor and the other Blue Team member in the race (who was coming in last, of course) collided, but neither of *them* was hurt.

Jay wasn't so lucky, though.

"Don't move him," the doctor told the teachers. Then he said to the kids who were crowding around, "Stand back. Let him have some air." And he sent Mr Cheney to call an ambulance

while he and Mr George eased Jay on to a
stretcher and moved him to the lodge.

Jay had broken his ankle. No one could really
concentrate on the race after that. Rick's team
halfheartedly beat mine.

The Blue Team had lost the event and the
Winter War.

I couldn't believe it.

"This didn't happen," I said to Stacey when it
was all over and we were walking back to the
lodge. "We didn't lose."

"I'm a little more concerned about Jay than the
war," Stacey replied crisply.

"But you hardly know Jay," I pointed out.

Stacey gave me a Look.

The truth is, I was worried about Jay myself. I just didn't want to admit it. I knew the accident was my fault. I was responsible for it. If I hadn't pushed Jay so hard he would never have entered the cross-country ski event. But I'd pushed, and Jay had entered, and he'd fallen and broken his ankle. I supposed that everyone blamed me for it.

All of a sudden I knew I was going to do something I don't do very often—cry. I quickened my pace, pulled ahead of Stacey, and rushed into the lodge.

"Hey, where are you going?" Stacey called after me.

I couldn't answer her. I just kept going, moving faster and faster towards our room, all the time thinking what a horrible person I was.

By the time I reached our room, a huge lump had formed in my throat, and my eyes were brimming with tears. I sincerely wished that no one would be in the dormitory.

I didn't get my wish.

Mary Anne was helping two of the children take off their mittens and boots and plastic bags. Wet clothing was draped everywhere—over chairs and beds and on the windowsills.

Luckily, Mary Anne took one look at me and saw that I was in trouble. She whisked Joey and Ian out of the room, sat me on the lower bunk, and said, "I suppose we lost the war, didn't we?"

I nodded numbly. "But that's not the worst

part," I managed to say. In between a lot of gulping and hiccupping, I told her about Jay Marsden.

"Well, that's pretty bad," Mary Anne said slowly, "but you know, you didn't *force* Jay to compete. He could have said no. He just *let* you push him into it."

"I do push people around, don't I?"

Mary Anne paused. At last she replied, "Well, you're a lot better about it than you used to be."

"Sometimes I just don't understand myself," I told her. "Usually I'm totally competitive—but there are times when I can force myself not to be. Like with the Krushers." (The Krushers are a team of children that I coach in softball.) "I hardly ever push them around, even when we have a game coming up. I tell them that the point of a game is just to have fun. That should have been the point of the Winter War, Mary Anne. Maybe . . . maybe I get more competitive when I'm taking part myself."

"Maybe," agreed Mary Anne. Then she gave me a hug.

"The kids all hate me," I told her with a sob.

"I doubt that," said Mary Anne.

As it turned out, she was right.

21st CHAPTER

Mallory ⚓

Friday evening

I'm sorry, but to be perfectly honest, I have to tell you that for a few brief, crazy moments, I hoped that because of Jay's accident, the all-school dance would be called off for some reason. You know, like in sympathy—— Jay couldn't dance, so we wouldn't, either. Not only did that not happen (**rats!**), but Jay was back at the lodge and in fine shape by dinnertime. The break had turned out not to be serious. Just two small bones were fractured, but I **suppose** you already know that, Mary Anne. Anyway, although I was glad to see Jay, I knew that I was going to start some major worrying. And I did....

I hoped for *anything* that would cancel the dance. I hoped the grand ballroom would burn down. I hoped the whole lodge would burn down. I hoped we'd all develop malaria.

"Jessi, Jessi, I'm going crazy," I said hysterically.

It was after dinner on Friday, and the stupid old all-school dance was supposed to start in less than an hour. Why hadn't the lodge burned down yet? I wondered. I'd wished hard enough for it.

"What's the matter?" asked Jessi.

"What's the matter? What's the *matter*? The dance is what's the matter."

Jessi looked at me blankly. I hadn't told her or anyone else my fears about the dance.

"It's—it's—I don't—I can't—"

"Mal, for heaven's sake, calm down. You're scaring the children," said Jessi.

The members of the BSC were returning to our dormitory to get ready for the dance, and the Conway Cove children were trickling in behind us.

I drew in a deep breath. Then I let it out slowly. "The dance. I've never been to one. I don't know how to dance. I didn't bring any good clothes with me. I'm going to make a fool of myself. Why can't it be Saturday already? Then we'd be home. The dance would be over. Well, I don't *really* want to leave Hooksett Crossing. This week has been fun. But—"

191

"Mallory," Jessi interrupted. "I've never been to a dance, either, but I'm looking forward to this one."

"That's because you can dance."

Jessi made a face. "I'm a *ballerina*. I can assure you that no one will be doing ballet steps tonight. However, if you would relax a little, you could dance perfectly well. Anybody can. Here." Jessi turned to Claud, who was looking into a mirror, carefully applying mascara to her eyelashes. "Claud, where's your cassette player? Can I borrow it for a sec?" she asked.

"Of course," replied Claud. She handed it to Jessi, who looked through Claudia's tape collection, chose a tape, and slipped it into the player.

When the music came on, Jessi said, "Okay, watch me and then imitate what I'm doing."

Jessi began moving around, snapping her fingers.

I tried to imitate her, I really did, but Jessi stepped forward, put her hands on my shoulders, and said sternly. "*Relax*. You look as though you're being carried off to gaol. This is just a dance."

I tried again . . . and again. At last Jessi said, "Much better! See? That wasn't so hard, was it?"

"No," I admitted. But then I added, "I didn't bring a dress. I haven't got anything to wear."

"Mallory, neither does anyone else. None of us knew about this dance until two days ago.

They've never had an all-school dance here before."

I was about to say, "Then how come Claudia has mascara with her?" when I remembered that she wears it almost every day. "Oh, yes," was all I said.

"So are you ready to get dressed?" asked Jessi. "Wear your red-and-white sweater with your jeans. That's a nice outfit."

"All right," I agreed.

The rest of my friends were trying to get ready, too, but it wasn't easy. Not with sixteen children hanging around. Most of them were watching us. The others were dancing to the music, which was still playing on Claud's cassette player. They were copying what they'd seen Jessi show me—and they weren't bad!

That was what gave me the idea. I suddenly thought, I bet the children would enjoy the dance. Then something else occurred to me. I ran over to Kristy (since she *is* the president of the Babysitters Club) and I said, "Hey, Kristy, what are the children going to do while everyone else is at the dance? We can't leave them alone."

"Gosh! I can't believe I didn't think of that," said Kristy, although *I* could believe it. She'd been totally distracted ever since Jay broke his ankle.

"I suppose Miss Weber or Mr Dougherty will take care of them."

"I—I think the children would rather go to the dance," I ventured.

"You do? But—"

"I'd be happy to look after them," I rushed on.

From nearby, Jessi frowned at me. She knew exactly what I was doing. If I had to look after the children, then it wouldn't matter if no one asked me to dance. I could just tell myself it was because I looked too busy. Besides, the children would probably have the time of their lives. They could drink punch and eat cakes. Everyone at the lodge thinks they're adorable anyway.

Of course, Kristy didn't know what was going through my head, so she said, "Sounds good to me. Ask Miss Halliday and Miss Weber and Mr Dougherty if it's okay with them."

So I did and it was. Their teachers even said I could be in charge. I think they were looking forward to the dance themselves. (Well, Miss Halliday was. I had a feeling the other two just wanted to go to bed early. They'd looked tired ever since they'd come back from hospital.)

As soon as I had the teachers' permission, I ran back to our dormitory. "Guess what!" I announced to the Conway Cove children. "You're going to the dance too!"

"We are?" they exclaimed.

"Great!" cried Ginnie.

"Will there be food?" asked Bryce.

"Definitely," I replied.

"We'd better get dressed!" said Pinky.

"Oh, you look fine the way you are."

"No, we want to look *good*," said Ian.

So the children went about making themselves look *good*. From out of nowhere appeared hair ribbons and plastic necklaces. Joey had even brought a clip-on bowtie. (I got the feeling he hadn't done his own packing.) Then followed a flurry of hair-brushing and shoe-polishing.

"Are you lot ready?" Dawn asked when things had died down.

"Yes," replied Ian. "And," he added, eyeing his classmates critically, "we look *good*."

"Yes. Good enough for a grown-up dance," said Pinky.

"Then let's go!" said Claud.

"Wait!" cried Mary Anne. "I want a picture of you children."

"Okay!" they said eagerly.

Mary Anne lined up the children in two rows against a backdrop of bunk beds. *Click* went her camera.

Then Pinky said, "How about a picture of you? Our babysitters. We haven't got a camera with us, but if I used your camera, Mary Anne, could you send us the picture later?"

Well, I could just about *see* Mary Anne melt. She nearly became a puddle on the floor of the dormitory. And I didn't blame her. *Pinky* wanted

195

a picture of *us*. She must have been getting over her homesickness.

Anyway, Mary Anne handed the camera to Pinky, Joey busily posed us, and *click* went the camera for a second time.

Then we were off to the dance.

My knees were actually shaking as we walked into the ballroom. Then I remembered that I had a job. The children. I tried herding them over to the refreshment table, but the punch and cakes didn't hold their attention for long.

"Let's dance," said Ginnie to Kara and Amber. "Everyone else is."

That wasn't true. But with so many kids and teachers in the grand ballroom, it looked as though the whole world was dancing. Before I knew what was happening, my charges were all out on the dance floor. Ryan danced with Miss Halliday, Valerie danced with Rick Chow, the captain of the Red Team. Renée, Corey, Kathie, Frankie, and Ian danced in a group.

I looked around helplessly.

My mouth dropped open. Jessi was dancing with a seventh-grade boy!

Then—to my astonishment—Curtis swayed by. In his arms was a waitress from the dining room. Curtis was looking at her lovingly. At that moment I knew that Curtis was definitely no killer. He was just the old cook . . . and he was in love.

I stood by the punch bowl for what seemed like hours. Yes, this was the dance nightmare of the century. Everyone else looked so uninhibited— The Conway Cove children, the teachers, my friends, the people who worked at the lodge. Why couldn't I—

"Excuse me, do you want to dance?"

I was startled back to reality. A boy was standing in front of me. I recognized him. He was in my maths class. Or maybe I'd just seen him in the cafeteria. Anyway, I was pretty sure he was in my grade. But he couldn't possibly be talking to me. I turned round. No one was behind me.

"I meant *you*," said the boy.

"Me?"

He nodded. "I'm Justin Price. We have maths together."

I tried to smile. "Oh . . . Right. I'm—"

"I know. You're Mallory Pike. Come on, let's dance."

I let Justin pull me into the crowd. I tried to remember everything Jessi had shown me, but pretty soon I realized that it didn't matter much. The room was so crowded that no one was paying attention to anyone else.

Justin and I spent the rest of the evening together. I stepped on his feet four times and he didn't mind at all.

Why had I ever worried about the dance?

22nd CHAPTER

Stacey

Friday night

Mary Anne, I hope you don't mind if I don't tell you everything about the dance. Some parts are just too personal. I'll tell you as much as I can, though.

I suppose it was no secret that Pierre and I wanted to spend the whole evening together. It was probably going to be the last time we'd see each other so we wanted the night to be special. Too bad we didn't know about the dance before we left for Hooksett Crossing. If we had, I would have brought along a special outfit. Oh, well. What really mattered was Pierre and me....

I'm not sure how it feels to be in love with a boy. Do you feel as though you want to be with him every second? As though you and he are the only two people in the world? As though you've known each other all your lives, even though you've just met? . . . As though your heart will break if you have to say goodbye to him?

If the answer to these questions is yes, then I was in love with Pierre, and had been since I first met him. It was a wonderful feeling, but scary too. As soon as I met Pierre, I was afraid I'd lose him.

One of the nice things about Pierre was that I could talk to him the same way I could talk to my friends in the Babysitters Club. We could tell each other about our feelings—about times when we'd been hurt or we were frightened, or about our feelings for each other. So I knew, Pierre was wondering if he was in love with me, just like I was wondering if I was in love with him. We'd talked about it. But we didn't have any answers.

Who would have thought that falling in love could be so hard?

Anyway, Pierre and I knew that Friday night would probably be the last time we'd spend any meaningful moments together. We'd say goodbye on Saturday, of course, but that wouldn't really count. It would be a hectic mess, and besides, tons of people would be around. Then the buses would leave, and Pierre would go back to Vermont and I would go back to Connecticut. There would be hours between us. We knew there wasn't much chance that we'd see each other again. We wouldn't even be coming back to the lodge the next winter.

I couldn't decide whether to look forward to the dance. On the one hand, it would be our last chance to be together. On the other hand, it would be our *last chance* to be *together*. Is that what is meant by "bittersweet"?

I made myself look as nice as possible for the dance, considering that my wardrobe consisted mostly of trousers and ski sweaters. Luckily, I had some make-up and jewellery with me, though. I managed to end up looking passable, particularly after I borrowed some fancy hair clips from Claudia. Anyway, Pierre hadn't seen me in anything dressy all week, so what did one more night matter?

Well, I suppose I ought to get straight to the dance now and the juicy parts. By the time my friends and I led the Conway Cove children down to the grand ballroom, the dance had already started. Most of the other kids were there, and Pierre was hanging around the entrance, waiting for me.

"Hi," I said softly.

"Hi," he replied. And before I knew it, we were in each other's arms, dancing across the floor.

We really wanted to spend the entire evening that way, but we knew it would be rude to look too exclusive, so we tried to swap partners every now and then. We also tried hard not to think about the awful thing that was going to happen the next day.

When we'd been at the dance for about an hour I said, "Pierre? Can we stop for a bit? I'm getting tired. And thirsty."

"Of course," he answered.

We made our way to the punch table, which wasn't easy since the room was so crowded. As we squeezed between couples and dodged arms and legs, I noticed a few interesting things. I pointed them out to Pierre after he'd got some punch for us and we were standing near the table, just watching people and enjoying being together.

"Look," I said. "There's Mallory, and she's *dancing*. With a *boy*!"

Pierre had spent hardly any time with my friends, but he knew all about them because we'd talked so much.

"Her first dance with a boy?" Pierre asked me.

I nodded. "She was so nervous tonight that she almost didn't come."

I kept watching the crowd. "There's Pinky," I said.

"Which one?"

"The little child dancing with Jessi. A few

202

minutes ago she was dancing with Mr George. She's really relaxed."

"I hope those children had fun this week," said Pierre.

"You know, I think they did—once they got over the shock of the accident. I mean, they've been pretty active. They've been skiing and skating and sledging. And I think they built every single snowman that's out on the lawn."

Pierre smiled. Then he frowned and leaned forward, peering into the crowd.

"What? What is it?" I asked.

"There's a child on crutches dancing with one of your friends."

"Where?"

"There." Pierre pointed.

"Oh, my gosh! That's Kristy and Jay!" I explained to Pierre who Jay was. "Kristy felt awfully guilty this afternoon."

"Jay looks like a twit," Pierre commented.

"Oh, he isn't," I answered, giggling. "He's nice. It took guts to go out there and dance on crutches, and even more guts to do it in order to show Kristy that he doesn't blame her for—uh-oh."

Now it was Pierre's turn. "What? What?"

"There's Guy and his whole family. Even the baby. Oh, I hope Claudia doesn't see them. She'll—Oops. Too late. She just saw them. And

203

Guy saw her. Oh, he's handing the baby to his wife. Now he's walking over to Claudia."

"He's cutting in on that boy she's dancing with," added Pierre.

"Now Claud and Guy are dancing. Ahh! That's nice. Claud looks as though she's died and gone to heaven."

Pierre and I finished our punch and began dancing again. We could hardly believe it when the lights dimmed so that the room was almost dark, and Mr George spoke into a microphone:

"This will be the last dance," he announced. "Mrs George and I hope you've enjoyed the evening and your stay at Leicester Lodge."

Everyone cheered and clapped loudly, then grew silent as a dreamy slow number began. Pierre and I swayed back and forth, and I felt happy and safe with his arms around me.

"This is it," Pierre whispered to me, and his breath tickled my ear.

I knew what he meant. It was our last dance together. Time to say goodbye. But I wasn't sure I was ready for that.

"Do we *have* to say goodbye?" I asked, hoping I wasn't whining.

"No." His breath was tickling my ear again. "Then let's not."

"Okay. Are we going to write to each other?"

"Maybe. Do you think there's any point?"

"Of course I do!"

I smiled and pulled myself even closer to
Pierre. "Okay. Then let's exchange addresses
tonight. Tomorrow will be too hard. I'd hate to do
it in a big crowd of people who are all exchanging
addresses, too."

"Yes," Pierre agreed.

A few minutes later I wrote my address on the
back of Pierre's hand, and he wrote his on mine.
Then he kissed me gently and walked away.

I decided I would never wash my hand again.

EPILOGUE

Mary Anne

And so we returned safely to Stoneybrook. Boy, was saying goodbye hard. And we had so many goodbyes to say. Everyone wanted to say goodbye to the Georges. The members of the BSC said goodbye to the Conway Cove kids and to Miss Weber and Mr. Dougherty, and they all said goodbye to us. Most of the little kids cried, and so did I, of course. Then Claudia had to find Guy to say goodbye to him and his family. The funny thing is, I didn't see Stacey and Pierre say goodbye ...

As I mentioned in the book for Logan, we arrived home safely. The roads were clear by Saturday, and the weather was sunny and bright, so there were no incidents on the way home—unless you count the boys on our coach singing a very unkind song once too often and causing a teacher on board to yell at them so loudly his dentures fell out. The boys were singing a song that's supposed to go like this:

> *"Alice, where are you going?"*
> *"Upstairs to take a bath."*
> *Alice, with legs like toothpicks*
> *and a neck like a giraffe.*
> *Alice got in the bathtub*
> *Alice pulled out the plug.*
> *Oh, my goodness! Bless my soul!*
> *There goes Alice down the hole!*
> *"Alice, where are you going?"*
> *"To . . . the . . . floor!"*

However, the boys were singing about Ethel Tines, the fat girl on the coach, and they'd changed the words of the song:

> *"Ethel, where are you going?"*
> *"Upstairs to take a bath."*
> *Ethel, with legs like tree stumps*
> *and a neck like a baboon.*
> (So it didn't rhyme.)

207

Mary Anne

> *Ethel got in the bathtub*
> *Ethel pulled the plug.*
> *Oh, my goodness! Bless my soul!*
> *Ethel can't fit down the hole!*

(They didn't have an end to this version, and it was probably just as well. However, the song didn't prevent Ethel from eating three Snickers bars on the way home.)

Anyway, we finally reached Stoneybrook, and I was so glad to see my father and Tigger again. We had a happy reunion, and Tigger purred practically nonstop all Saturday evening.

A couple of weeks after we'd been back, the members of the BSC started receiving mail. Here are some of the postcards:

Dear Jessi,
    Hi. How are you? I read the book you told me about. The one called Pinky Pye. I liked it because the kitten had my name.
                    Love, Pinky
P.S. Thank Mary Anne for the photo she sent. My friends and I like it.

Mary Anne

DEAR STACEY,
   SEE? I TOLD YOU WE'D WRITE.
THANK YOU FOR YOUR LETTER. I'LL
NEVER FORGET OUR WEEK AT THE LODGE,
EITHER. IT WAS THE BEST ONE OF MY
LIFE. I LOVE YOU.
      -- BILL (JUST KIDDING. THIS IS
         ME, PIERRE, OF COURSE.)

(I'm not sure I would write "I love you" on a
postcard where the postman and your mother
could see it.)

Dear Claud,
   Hi! How's it going? How was the lodge? Are
you coming to Camp Mohawk again this
summer? You never did let me know.
I'm going back. Even if you don't go,
promise me you'll wear those stupid
teepee clothes for two weeks out of
sympathy for me.
                     Love, Will

My Dear Claudia,
   Hello from Leicester Lodge! Marie
asked about you this morning. I

209

told her we would probably not see such a marvellous skier as you for a long time. However, Marie is turning into quite a skier. She went down a beginner trail by herself the other day. Domitille sends her love.

-- Guy

Some important things happened after we got home again:

1. Kristy got over losing the Winter War.
2. Kristy stopped feeling guilty about Jay.
3. Kristy and Claudia stopped being angry with each other.
4. Jay had his plaster cast taken off.
5. My dad and Dawn's mum went to a formal dance together.
6. I finished my project on time, handed it in, and got a grade A for it.
7. I collected the notes my friends had been keeping at the lodge and finished my book for Logan.

I suppose the most important news of all was that Logan and I were happily reunited the day after we got back from Vermont. Actually, the reunion was probably more soppy than happy. Dad and I drove to the airport to pick up the Brunos, and as soon as I saw Logan, I ran straight into his arms. He had bought a coral necklace for me in Aruba and had it ready so that while I was hugging him, he fastened it around my neck. Then we held hands all the way home.

Logan's little brother kept looking at us and saying, "Ugh! Ugh!"

Twelve days later, I finished Logan's book. It had taken longer to write than I'd expected. I had to do a lot of editing. I realized I needed to take out all the parts about my wondering if Logan had found a new girlfriend, and about the daft letters I kept writing to him.

At last the book was finished, though. I illustrated it as best I could (I'm not much of an artist), bound it (with Claudia's help), and presented it to Logan.

He loved it.

Oh, yes. One other thing. This is the dedication in the front of the book:

For Kristy, Dawn, Claudia,
Stacey, Jessi, and Mal—
the greatest friends
in the world.

MYSTERY THRILLERS

Introducing a new series of hard-hitting action-packed thrillers for young adults.

THE SONG OF THE DEAD by Anthony Masters
For the first time in years "the song of the dead" is heard around Whitstable. Is it really the cries of dead sailors? Or is it something more sinister? Barney Hampton is determined to get to the bottom of the mystery . . .

THE FERRYMAN'S SON by Ian Strachan
Rob is convinced that Drewe and Miles are up to no good. Where do they go on their night cruises? And why does Kimberley go with them? When Kimberley disappears Rob finds himself embroiled in a web of deadly intrigue . . .

TREASURE OF GREY MANOR by Terry Deary
When Jamie Williams and Trish Grey join forces for a school history project, they unearth much more than they bargain for! The diary of the long-dead Marie Grey hints at the existence of hidden treasure. But Jamie and Trish aren't the only ones interested in the treasure – and some people don't mind playing dirty . . .

THE FOGGIEST by Dave Belbin
As Rachel and Matt Gunn move into their new home, a strange fog descends over the country. Then Rachel and Matt's father disappears from his job at the weather station, and they discover the sinister truth behind the fog . . .

BLUE MURDER by Jay Kelso
One foggy night Mack McBride is walking along the pier when he hears a scream and a splash. Convinced that a murder has been committed he decides to investigate and finds himself in more trouble than he ever dreamed of . . .

DEAD MAN'S SECRET by Linda Allen
After Annabel's Uncle Nick is killed in a rock-climbing accident, she becomes caught up in a nerve-wracking chain of events. Helped by her friends Simon and Julie, she discovers Uncle Nick was involved in some very unscrupulous activities . . .

CROSSFIRE by Peter Beere
After running away from Southern Ireland Maggie finds herself roaming the streets of London destitute and alone. To make matters worse, her step-father is an important member of the IRA – if he doesn't find her before his enemies do, she might just find herself caught up in the crossfire . . .

THE THIRD DRAGON by Garry Kilworth
Following the massacre at Tiananmen Square Xu flees to Hong Kong, where he is befriended by John Tenniel, and his two friends Peter and Jenny. They hide him in a hillside cave, but soon find themselves swept up in a hazardous adventure that could have deadly results . . .

VANISHING POINT by Anthony Masters
In a strange dream. Danny sees his father's train vanishing into a tunnel, never to be seen again. When Danny's father really does disappear, Danny and his friend Laura are drawn into a criminal world, far more deadly than they could ever have imagined . . .

GREEN WATCH by Anthony Masters

BATTLE FOR THE BADGERS

Tim's been sent to stay with his weird Uncle Seb and his two kids, Flower and Brian, who run Green Watch – an environmental pressure group. At first Tim thinks they're a bunch of cranks – but soon he finds himself battling to save badgers from extermination . . .

SAD SONG OF THE WHALE

Tim leaps at the chance to join Green Watch on an anti-whaling expedition. But soon, he and the other members of Green Watch, find themselves shipwrecked and fighting for their lives . . .

DOLPHIN'S REVENGE

The members of Green Watch are convinced that Sam Jefferson is mistreating his dolphins – but how can they prove it? Not only that, but they must save Loner, a wild dolphin, from captivity . . .

MONSTERS ON THE BEACH

The Green Watch team is called to investigate a suspected radiation leak. Teddy McCormack claims to have seen mutated crabs and sea-plants, but there's no proof, and Green Watch don't know whether he's crazy or there's been a cover-up . . .

GORILLA MOUNTAIN

Tim, Brian and Flower fly to Africa to meet the Bests, who are protecting gorillas from poachers. But they are ambushed and Alison Best is kidnapped. It is up to them to rescue her *and* save the gorillas . . .

SPIRIT OF THE CONDOR

Green Watch has gone to California on a surfing holiday – but not for long! Someone is trying to kill the Californian Condor, the bird cherished by an Indian tribe – the Daiku – without which the tribe will die. Green Watch must struggle to save both the Condor and the Daiku . . .

POINT HORROR

Introducing a new series of horror fiction for young adults
– read them if you dare!

APRIL FOOLS by Richie Tankersley Cusick
Driving back from a party on April 1st Belinda, Frank and
Hildy are involved in a gruesome accident. Thinking no
one could have survived, they run away from the scene.
But someone must have survived the crash, and they're
going to make Belinda suffer for what happened . . .

TRICK OR TREAT by Richie Tankersley Cusick
From the beginning Martha knew there was something
evil about the house; something cold; something sinister.
Then the practical jokes begin, and she is sure someone is
following her . . .

MY SECRET ADMIRER by Carol Ellis
Jenny's parents go away leaving her alone in their new
house. Then the phonecalls start – Jenny has a secret
admirer who courts her with sweet messages, but she also
has an enemy who chases her on a lonely road. She has no
one to turn to except her secret admirer – but who is he? . . .

THE LIFEGUARD by Richie Tankersley Cusick
Kelsey's summer on Beverley Island should have been
paradise, but it quickly turns into a nightmare. It starts
with a message from a girl who's missing, and there have
been a number of suspicious drownings. At least the
lifeguards will protect her. Poor Kelsey. Someone forgot to
tell her that lifeguards don't always like to save lives . . .

BEACH PARTY by R.L. Stine
Karen plans to party all summer with her friend Ann-
Marie. The fun starts when she meets two new guys. But
which should she choose: handsome Jerry or dangerous
Vince? But the party turns nasty when the threats start.
Someone wants Karen to stay away from Jerry at all
costs . . .

FUNHOUSE by Diane Hoh

Everyone in Santa Luisa is horrified when the Devil Elbow's roller coaster flies off its rails. And no one believes Tess when she says she saw someone tampering with the track. But someone knows Tess is telling the truth – someone who is playing a deadly game, and Tess is in the way . . .

THE BABY-SITTER by R.L. Stine

From the moment that Jenny accepts the Hagen baby-sitting job, she knows she's made a terrible mistake. The Hagen house fills her with horror, and she finds a creepy "neighbour" prowling in the back yard. Then the crank phonecalls start – but who wants to hurt her? What kind of maniac is willing to scare her . . . to death? . . .

Look out for:
Teacher's Pet by Richie Tankersley Cusick
The Boyfriend by R.L. Stine